Blood
In The Water

◆

Fishing Tales
of the Islands

◆

M.N. Muench

Cover Art:

Fishermen Launching an Alia,

W.N. Witzell, 1972 ©

Disclaimer

This is a work of fiction. All similarity to persons, places, or events, of the past or present is purely coincidental.

Dedication

The author dedicates this collection of stories in memory of Alan Banner, U.S. Peace Corps Volunteer and Fisheries Biologist, lost at sea in a shark attack in 1972 while carrying out his Volunteer duties. He was a man at home with the oceans, an awesome fisherman, and an outstanding marine biologist. The world would be a better place had he not died so young. He is missed and fondly remembered. Much Aloha to you Al.

Acknowledgments

The author is deeply indebted to W.N. Witzell, NMFS Fisheries Research Biologist, returned U.S. Peace Corps Volunteer, and a close friend of over forty years, for his considerable input. Wayne made substantial recommendations on the stories appearing in this collection and patiently read many drafts; always gracious and encouraging in his comments and recommendations. It was a true test and proof, of his friendship. Words cannot fully express my gratitude.

This work moved from a collection of Word files to book format largely due to the encouragement of Pete Martinez, friend, running buddy, and confidant, who never let me forget the task demanded completion. Pete, now deceased, had the ability to mix humor and impatience in a masterful way, and I could not help but conquer the endless difficulties before me. His words continue to influence. He was a good friend and is deeply missed.

I also extend my thanks to Don Fallis, my good friend and Ultra running compatriot, who was always ready to read story drafts and offer sound criticism, while providing a bounty of good-natured support and encouragement.

These fine gentlemen contributed to the quality of this collection, while any failures, technical or otherwise, are solely the responsibility of the author.

Contents

Blood in the Water   ...   1

Night Fishing   ...   31

Fishermen   ...   41

Boat Anchor   ...   51

Archimedes Fish Fry   ...   71

By Hook and Line   ...   103

Blood in the Water

"Birds!" cried Sione, "There!" he screamed as he stood at the bow of the small boat and pointed off to the starboard quarter. Aleki threw the twenty-four foot fishing boat into a wide turn and it heeled into the rising blue swell. The black specks in the direction of Sione's pointing arm moved slowly up the starboard gunwale and toward the bow as the boat surged down the rolling sea. The horizon filled with the next swell as it rose high before them. They pushed on, waiting to crest it, to take another look toward the working birds.

"Many?" called Aleki excitedly from his position at the outboard in the stern.

"Yes! Working!" answered Sione, fighting to keep his balance as the boat roller-coastered through the ten-foot swell. Sione had the best eyes in the boat and was standing in the bow acting as lookout.

All morning long they had run a game of hide-and-seek with large schools of mostly skipjack tuna and yellow-fin, with bonito, rainbow runners, and dolphins mixed in. They were reaping a great bounty, had managed to stay near the schools, keeping the time between action to a minimum. It had been a matter of good fortune and teamwork. Aleki had developed the intuition to guess the direction of the next rising, and Sione had been quick to see the working birds. The result was a bilge filled with two to twenty pound fish; a magnificent catch and sure to bring in a good profit for the four men aboard. The boat rose to the top of a swell as Sione stood, hanging onto the anchor line with one hand and pointing off to the port with the other. Aleki adjusted the course and the boat plunged down the back of the swell and toward the bottom of the trough.

The other men in the boat were busy with their own tasks. Lafo, who sat to starboard amidships, was furiously working at a great tangle of line. Ioane, who sat next to him, bent toward the stern, bailer in hand, waiting for the rush of bloody bilge water to surge back as the boat climbed the opposite wall of the swell. There was a tense pleasant excitement running through the crew. Each knew the minutes between contacts were as critical as the brief moments of frantic action occurring as they swung through a feeding school. Lafo worked the two lines quickly in and out of the tangles. It was serious business. All lines would have to be in the water when they hit the school. With two lines tangled they would cut their strikes by half, and it was likely they would have only one or two passes before the school sounded or outran the boat. Then it would be long loops around a vacant ocean as Aleki and Sione searched to find another sign of working birds.

The boat hit the bottom of the swell. The motor changed pitch as water surged against the stern and reached the exhaust manifold and the strain of climbing the opposing face dragged at the prop. Looking back across the watery valley, Ioane could see the zigzag light blue ribbon of bubbles churned up by the prop. As the boat rode up the wave the stern filled with bloodied water and scum, and he bailed furiously. As they cut across the crest, a burst of cool spray rode the stiff breezes, adding to the layers of dried sweat and salt caked on their skins.

"There!" screamed Sione just as the boat started its rapid fall through the next trough.

"Many?" yelled Aleki. "How far?"

"Many! Not far. Soon!"

"Lafo get those lines untangled. Ioane help him!" ordered Aleki. Ioane dropped the bailer and looked at Lafo, who handed him one of the lures. The extra hands made quick work of the last of the tangles in the lines. Sione stood as the boat crested the swell, and Aleki did the same. Lafo and Ioane had each payed out the mother-of-pearl shell lures a good five to ten yards behind the boat. A few hundred yards away a whirling mass of brown foot boobies, terns, shearwaters, and frigate birds circled and cried, diving wildly into the water, rising, and diving again.

Aleki grabbed his line, threw the spindle into the bilge and guided the line out over the stern with his left hand as he held the long wooden handcrafted tiller bar between his knees. The spindle bounced around the bottom of the boat as he alternately pulled at the line and let lengths of it pay out. Meanwhile, Sione had let his line out on the starboard side of the boat. Pandemonium erupted as the boat reached the birds. The water started to boil with thousands of fish forming the upper layer of a school extending as far down into the clear blue water as the eye could see. Shiny underbellies and glistening heads sparkled everywhere in the deep. Fish jumped so close to the boat the men could have touched them if they had not been so intent on their lines. Hundreds of birds from a half dozen species circled, screeching, hovering, and then falling among waves of bait spattering the water like sheets of driving rain.

"*Sau i'a!*" (Come fish!), screamed Aleki.

"*Maua!*" (Caught!), screamed Lafo as he pulled madly at his line.

"*Ua sau i'a!*" (The fish comes!) laughed Ioane as his line went taut. At the same instant a fish rose to the surface behind the boat, occasionally skipping along the water, then sounding, and taking the line off at a greater angle. Ioane was in a frantic tug-o-war, straining to pull in handfuls line looping haphazardly onto the floorboards. The thick line cut at his hands as the fish fought to escape. The nylon lay in piles all about the bilges catching on fish, sharp corners, gear, tangling in on itself and shuffling in with Lafo's line. Lafo sat to port battling his own fish, creating another chaos. They glanced at each other grinning wildly, arms straining to land their fighting catches.

Forward, Sione felt a strike, the line going rigid in his hands. He cursed when just moments later it went slack again, the fish slipping the hook, and almost instantly, he cackled loudly as another fish hit. This one heavy on the line.

Fish boiled out of the water around the boat, jumping after bait spraying the surface in long waves of fear, like sheets of driving rain. Birds screamed, dove at fish, bait, and occasionally picked up lures. The men howled maniacally, laughed, and cursed as they bathed in the excitement of the hunt. Blood sprayed about the boat, its

4

origin uncertain. There was utter chaos as dozens of species sought to feed.

Aleki tugged madly at his line, occasionally grabbing it in his teeth and was often forced to steer the boat with the tiller bar between his knees. Lafo landed a ten-pound skipjack. It leaped wildly about the bilge as he laughed and yelled, trying to pin it to the floorboards, so he could free the hook. Blood flew from its mouth and gills, splashing over the insides of the boat, covering Lafo's legs and arms in crimson ribbons of slime.

Moments later, just as Lafo managed to get his fish pinned against the bulwarks, Ioane landed his. It danced around on the end of the line, flapping and jerking, spurts of blood spattering the bilges. Still living bait flew from its mouth. A spine poked into Lafo's leg as he worked the hook out, and he growled painfully at the battling fish. With slimy bloodied hands, he tossed his line over again—only to find Ioane's fish had tangled in piles of his line. Cursing the convulsing beast, he grabbed a wooden club and started beating madly at the fish, whacking the floor and nearly breaking Ioane's toe as the fish instinctively avoided the blows of the heavy club. After a few good whacks at the fish, the near insane men ripped the hook out and worked frantically to get the lines back into the school.

Just as they solved the tangle, Aleki pulled his fish up to the boat, and Ioane reached out and gaffed the fish, pulling it aboard. Larger than the others, it flexed and sprung madly about the stern as Ioane beat it with the handle of the gaff. The hook slipped. The line was thrown back, the men ignoring the newly caught fish, which continued to choke up bubbly blood, yellow ooze, and pieces of baitfish while they concentrated on the hunt.

Almost as fast as the lures were over the side they were hit again. All four men pulled madly, screaming wildly, laughing, and riding the adrenalin high of predation to the limits of their physical strength. The killing filled them and kept them keyed as they fought to land their catch.

Ioane's lure was a few feet behind the boat when it was struck, pulled his fish aboard, picked up a short club and beat it silent, all the time cussing, screaming, and happy.

"Lafo! Here!" yelled Aleki as he passed him his own taut line. Aleki was busy trying to find the school, which had sounded. He, like the birds, circled bewildered. Two fish hit the lines, the mad excitement ebbed quickly leaving them breathing violently and stunned.

Sione shortened his line and stood in the slightly rolling boat. The birds had already scattered. The ocean was empty. They pushed a bit bewildered across the rolling swells, looking for the school of fish.

"How many?" asked Aleki.

"Two," said Ioane.

"Two," said Sione.

"Three," added Lafo.

"And I got two," said Aleki. "Sione how many in the boat?"

Sione looked toward the front of the boat where the fish lay piled under the foredeck and in a box sitting in front of the thwart. "Maybe thirty, could be forty. Time to head back," he said looking at the sun. "It is late."

6

"We are catching fish!" said Aleki, unwilling to let go of the joyous madness.

"Yes," said Sione, looking off to the east, "and we have to sell these when we get in, and clean the boat, and load the truck. It will all take time. I want to be home in time for prayers!" he laughed. "How about you, Ioane? Do you want your wife to say the blessing tonight, or are you satisfied with today's catch?"

"There is another day," said Ioane, who did not want to sound like he was opposing Aleki. He was tired. The work had been strenuous, the sun hot, and he was never comfortable fishing this far out, preferring fishing inside the reef from a small outrigger, where there were no swells, and one could see the bottom.

No one asked Lafo what he thought. If they had, he would have remained quiet. Hard work was hard work, and he expected to shoulder more than his share of it. In the boat, or at home, he would be bending his muscles to something until just before he went to sleep. He sat there, his head down, fiddling with a tangled line.

Aleki stared out toward the horizon. There were no birds in sight. Yet, how he wanted to continue the chase! He did not want it to stop. It was satisfying to have a good catch. The new boat and the motor made a great difference. He wanted to show the village how successful he could be.

He looked at the mountains of the island rising from the sea many miles to the south. Sione was right, however. As much as Aleki hated to admit it, Sione was a better fisherman than he. The day's work was not over, and there was much to do besides catch fish. Ioane was right too, there would be other days.

"Ok. It is good. We head back. Lafo get those fish forward, Ioane you get the lines put away," said Aleki as he looked at Sione and nodded his agreement. Aleki put the boat in a wide arc and headed it toward the hazy blue island. Sione helped Lafo pack the fish into burlap bags, and they pushed them between the two seats around the spare seven-horse motor stored there. Others he stuffed under a tarp pushed under the front foredeck. Assessing it all, Sione was concerned about the added weight of so much fish. The freeboard was down to less than four inches, and the swell would now be passing across their port stern quarter. It made for some tricky running back to the village. He trusted Aleki, who had learned much in the recent months, and who appeared a cautious man. Aleki had not been fishing long. He was starting to behave like a man who had. He took care of his boat and the motors, always brought supplies and back-up, and he was fair in his division of the catch. Sione noticed even Lafo received his full share, which was not often the case among the village chiefs who owned boats and hired crews for them.

Looking out over the rolling ocean and then down at the freeboard, he thought about asking Aleki if he wanted relief at the tiller. He had second thoughts, as he had already contradicted Aleki once. To do so again would only invite friction. He did not want to antagonize Aleki. He liked him. Instead, Sione sat quietly in the bow, rearranging the gear and trimming the boat. Looking off toward the island, he gauged it would be a two difficult hours before they reached the reefed lagoon of the village. The sun bore down on the boat as it made its way over the rolling seas, and now, the action over, its heavy warm weight caused the men to doze. The brightness and the salt caking their eyes caused them to blink, and each blink

8

became longer as weary muscles relaxed, and thoughts drifted toward pleasant expectations of cool showers and long rests. Sleep became a siren, beckoning, calling each one to the paradise of forgetfulness. On a long roll and pitch, Ioane lost his balance, keeling over into the bilge as the boat raced down a swell and hit a rouge chop. He climbed up sheepishly, met only mild smiles as the others could only be thankful the diversion had allowed them to set aside the heavy dullness slipping over their own minds.

"Lafo hand me the water," said Sione. Lafo passed him a jug and he took a few long swigs; washing down the pieces of the taro he had been chewing on intermittently. Looking at Aleki, he held up the jug, Aleki nodded, and Sione passed it to Lafo and pointed toward Aleki. Taking the jug, Aleki took a long pull. Its sweetness caressed his raw throat, and its revitalizing effect was immediate. Aleki looked around as he stood, the tiller between his knees. It was a strange sea washing past the stern of the boat; long rolling swells had quickly risen to at least fifteen feet. A chop was running out of the east, from just north of the swell. It was making handling the loaded boat difficult.

The boat now wallowed as it hit the bottom of a swell and wanted to crab, to turn broadside to the wind and sea. When it did, the engine lost power, and the seas would surge against transom as the swell overtook the boat. Aleki found he had to over-steer at the bottom of a trough and gun the engine to keep speed, to avoid the chance of broaching. Thinking it over as he rode down each swell and went through the actions repeatedly, he realized the boat was overloaded.

Shifting the weight would do little good. Sione had already arranged it so as much was amidships as possible. There was just too much weight aboard. Aleki could not see how he could lighten the load without cutting his crew, or catching fewer fish. He needed the extra motor, and he needed the tanks of fuel he carried. To go short one man could cut into the catch. It was not just one fewer line in the water; it was two fewer hands. He shook his head and wondered how he could do what the Fisheries Office people had told him was possible with this boat and engine.

The trip became long, and in his weariness Aleki found it difficult to concentrate on handling the boat. He could see the others drifting off and could only envy their leisure. He thought of asking Sione to take over for a while. He did not think it would be right. It was, after all, his boat and his responsibility. So, he fought against the curtain of exhaustion by talking to the others.

"Sione do you think we can sell the fish this side of Solosolo, or will we have to go into town?"

"Town, probably. I think we can sell some of this at the hotels and much along the way, at the major stores. No need for the afternoon market. This is quality catch. We should be able to set a good price and make only the best stops."

"How much money?"

"It depends on what will we keep," replied Sione, reluctant to talk sums of money.

Aleki mulled over Sione's response, for it contained much meaning.

What they kept was what did not go to the village. He had agreed with Sione before he bought the boat and motor, it was to be a business run on European rules and not by Island custom. They agreed contributions to the village were necessary; they just needed to limit the percentage they passed out to powerful chiefs, ministers, their families, friends, and others, to about twenty to thirty percent of the catch. The rest they would sell for cash, to pay expenses, with any profit divided among the crew by shares. What the men did with their money was up to them. It was a tough reality. When a boat landed, everyone in the village expected something. Aleki couldn't dealing well with the pressure. He left much of it to Sione, who, though of lesser title, had the political shrewdness of a long-standing *failauoga*, or talking chief. Sione could often politely talk their way out of town under the limits they had set. Aleki had to admit, coming home was, for him, the uncomfortable part of fishing.

Sione glanced off to the east as he felt the wind hitting the back of his neck. A squall line had come over the horizon and was rapidly heading their way. He figured it would quickly overtake them, long before they reached the safety of the reef. They could only wait and see. Twenty minutes later, the first of the towering gray clouds knotted angrily over a gray parallelogram of rain and raced to intercept them. The sea chop rose with freshening winds. Sione motioned to Aleki, who looked back toward the billowing clouds and nodded. They knew they would be in for a difficult time, and understood they must be cautious.

The winds rose for ten minutes, and gusts soon whipped the tops of the swells, causing them to break into foaming horses racing the boat down the swell. The sun still shone brightly to the west. Off to the northeast, the sky filled with the oncoming squall; a growing expanse of ugly clouds bound to the dark ocean by a black curtain of rain. The clear blue water quickly turned murky, then green, and deepened into a tarnished gunmetal gray as the clouds blotted out the sun. The temperature dropped rapidly, and the wind whipped spray slapped against the boat each time it surged off the top of a swell. The wind gusted, and scattered drops of rain pelted the water, the boat, and the men.

They searched the boat for the sweaters and jackets they had long since shed. The windblown spray, coupled with the sunburns of a long day's fishing, caused them to chill quickly, raising the hairs on their legs and arms, and bringing on unwelcome shivers. The rain fell steadily. Whipped by the wind, it beat the ocean frothy. Beads of driving rain stung the flesh, raising welts, and making it difficult to see, and each man sought protection as best he could. Ioane hid under a sheet of plastic, slumping down in the bilge, his back against the thwart. Lafo simply pulled his coconut frond hat down low over his forehead, and sat, the rain pelting him, waiting patiently for the squall to pass.

Aleki tied a yellow southwester to his head. It was still almost impossible to see. A watery curtain had descended between him and Sione in the bow. He was running the boat by feel; and looking back to gauge their position on the swells he was blinded by the driving rain. On one occasion, the boat crabbed before he expected it to, the engine lost thrust, and water surged over-the-transom as the boat was fighting onto the windward surface of the wave and overtaken by the following swell. He quickly gunned the engine, outracing the overwhelming surge and corrected the course. Though only a little water found its way into the boat, it sent a rush of fear from his groin. It showed him how close they were to mishap. Riding the back of another wave, he was alarmed to see the water in the bilge was to his ankles. Water cascaded down his face, blinding him, and forcing him to work the rudder by feel.

"Lafo! Ioane!" he yelled, urgently. "The bailers! Quick! Bail!"

Ioane picked up a bailer and turned to the rear of the boat. He scooped the water out of the bilge and threw it over the side. Each scoop caught in the wind, blowing right back at him. He switched sides, tossing the water to the lee. It was still miserable work. Ioane was rapidly feeling worse, his fear causing him to bail madly. Lafo saw their danger and bailed quickly. He passed no judgment on its effectiveness; it simply needed doing. He understood there was much futility in life and was resigned; having gotten in the boat, he could only work until he was out of it once again.

Sione, alerted by the yawing of the boat and the change in the pitch of the engine, looked to the stern in time to see the water surge over the transom. It was not much water, though a bad sign. Aleki had acted correctly. Yet it meant trouble. The squall was getting fierce, the wind was whipping up a chop, making it difficult to control the boat. The sea spray was blowing into the boat as quickly as the rain. If he had been at the tiller, he would have turned the boat around and headed back into the swell and wind. It was safer to run into a storm, though he felt it would cause too much confusion to try to get Aleki to do this now. He picked up a large coconut shell from the bilge and started scooping out the bloodied water. "With three working, maybe we can stay even," he thought hopefully.

The squall peaked, the wind gusted, and rain lashed the sea in sheets, whipping the choppy surface into a white froth that slid across the gray-blue marble sea, like snow over a frozen lake. Aleki steered blindly, water cascading down his face. He moved the tiller by the feel of the pitch and roll of the boat, and intuition. He could see nothing, even with his back to the wind. Ioane and Lafo, who were only a few feet from him, were blurry images. The water in the bilges rose above his ankles and then disappeared as they hurtled down the next ravine between high swells.

They hit the bottom of the trough heavily and he felt the bow bury, pulling up sluggishly. He gunned the engine as the weight of the water in the bilge drove the bow lower. The boat wanted to crab broadside to the swell. He pushed the tiller around, fighting to keep it running diagonally along the swell, revving the engine. Even at full throttle, the boat hesitated, and was slow in gaining momentum. The swell surged over the transom, broaching the boat, and five gallons of water poured in before Aleki could regain control and gun the engine, pushing the boat ahead of the following swell.

His bowels tightened as the water rushed back over his ankles. When they reached the crest, the full force of the storm beat the boat and lashed them with a stinging mixture of salt spray and rain. Then the boat slipped fast down the next ridge of the swell, almost out of control. The bow dug in as it hit bottom, sticking there, and rising from the water ever so slowly. Aleki gunned the engine as the bow shed water from the foredeck. They could not gain speed. The following swell came surging in over the transom in one long rush.

"Oh, God!" he pleaded silently. "Not now!" The motor refused to die! There was still a chance. "Bail!" he screamed into the wind, "Bail!"

Water sloshed just under the seats, while the others bailed frantically, making little progress. It surged through the boat as the engine fought to push the heavy boat up the next wave. Aleki was standing in water to his calves. There were only a few inches of inside freeboard remaining in the stern, and he bent quickly, frantically scooping water with his hand. The boat reached the top of the swell, rolled sickeningly, and moved sluggishly down the next incline. Aleki gunned the throttle, hoping to gain control. He threw the tiller over, hoping to avoid running straight down the wave. The weight of the boat made steering almost impossible and just carried the boat toward the bottom, where the bow buried with a soft jar. Water poured over the gunwales as the boat yawed into the now oncoming swell. In an instant, the transom was awash, the force of the driving swell pushing it deeper and deeper. The engine died as the air intake sucked saltwater.

Aleki realized he was holding the tiller, standing in water nearly to his waist and wondered if the boat was just going to disappear under him. It didn't. Slowly, like a breaching whale, it rose toward the surface, one gunwale slightly out of the water, and threatening to capsize.

"Down!" screamed Sione as he saw the others standing instinctively. "Get down or she'll roll over!" The men obeyed without question, sitting chest deep in water. "Ioane, grab the water jug!" he yelled as he saw the orange five-gallon jug floating away. Then everyone started looking around and grabbing at floating gear, on the verge of drifting away. They sat helplessly, the boat rolling sickeningly, gunwales alternately under water, the boat lying broadside to the swell.

The fury of the squall had suddenly passed, though the pelting rain continued. The sky brightened and the sea slowly turning a murky green. Exhausted, they sat in stunned silence.

"We must lighten the boat!" called Sione to Aleki. "We have to get it afloat again before the next squall. We must get rid of the fish and the spare motor! At least," he continued.

Aleki stared blankly as he slowly grasped Sione's words. Horrified, he screamed back, "You want to throw the fish and the seven-horse overboard? The motor cost me three hundred tala! It's almost new!" he protested. "And we will probably get two hundred tala for the fish! No! No Sione! There has to be a better way. We must think of something else!"

Sione stared at Aleki in disbelief, and with growing despair. "Aleki," he said, "we cannot get home like this! We must lighten the boat if we are to save it. Aleki," he continued in as calm a tone as he could manage, "there is much blood in the water. We must get rid of the fish before we have sharks. This is dangerous. We can still get home if we act correctly."

Perhaps Aleki was in shock, or it was guilt over his failure to keep the boat afloat. For whatever reason, he could not accept the thought of losing his catch, nor of pitching the spare motor overboard. In his mind, it did not make sense. What would he say to his family when he got

16

home? How could he explain the loss of the near new motor, which had cost them so dearly. The village would laugh at him if he came home empty-handed. He could only think these thoughts, could only see the terrible embarrassment of failure for his family and before the entire village. Unlike Sione who had spent much of his life fishing, he was still land bound. He had no great fear and at this desperate moment, could not understand all four men were close to death.

The fish then?" said Sione urgently. "Let us throw the fish overboard. Now," he continued, hoping at least to limit the risk of attracting sharks. To his horror, Aleki shook his head and sat there staring at him.

"Sione," said Aleki, "we just cannot just throw the day's catch over."

"Aleki, sharks will come, and we are more in the water than in the boat. It will be bad."

"You are just scared, I think. A shark may come. We are in the boat," said Aleki stressing the 'A'.

"Aleki I have seen sharks come when we bail bloody water on a good night of bottom fishing. I am afraid of them then, when I am in a dry boat! Scared you say? Yes, I am scared! What of Viliamu, Iosefa, and Ioane Lesa? They are all men of the district who have died fishing over the last year. Yes, Aleki, I am afraid. I see death, and you see failure. Believe me my friend. We will be lucky if we are all just failures at the end of this day!"

The words effected Aleki, and he was near accepting their precarious state. He was on the verge of throwing the catch overboard, when suddenly the sun broke through the clouds, and the day returned to an almost normal

17

state. The island was off to the south. The winds had moderated, and the sea calmed. The squall was rapidly retreating. It caused him to hesitate. For whatever reason, Aleki chose to view the passing of the squall as a good sign; an omen of better fortune, one suggesting they would find an answer allowing him to lose nothing in the bargain.

"No," he said looking at Sione.

Sione knew what he was going to do if Aleki refused. He dreaded his next decision. It was the only one left to him. When Aleki had said no, it became a choice between two death sentences. He knew the loaded boat was a certain invitation to disaster. By leaving the boat he might survive, though he figured he would die just the same.

"I'm not staying then," he said, looking sadly at Aleki. "I'll take this can," he continued, pointing to a ten-gallon gas can floating near him. "It is mine, and I'll need something to help me stay afloat." He reached over, grabbed the can and tied a short rope to it. "Can I have a drink of water before I go?" he asked looking at Aleki.

Aleki was stunned. Sione was talking crazy. It did not make sense. "You are not going to swim to shore, are you?"

"No, I'm probably not," said Sione voicing his deepest doubts. "I'm not going to stay here either. Can I have a drink?"

"Of course," said Aleki, and Sione untied the water jug and held it up to judge the weight and height of the water. He took a few gulps, held it up again, and took a few more. When he finished he had drunk a quarter of the water in the jug. He did not think they would be needing all the remaining water.

"If I make it before you, I will send help. You do the same, OK? Lafo, Ioane, good-bye and good luck," he said, nodding at the two men. "Aleki, I know you are doing what you think is right. You are mistaken. Good-bye, and may God be with you." Then Sione threw the gas can off the boat and fell into the water. He started swimming as rapidly as possible, kicking with his feet and pushing the can in front of him.

It happened so fast Aleki had no time to say anything. "Sione!" he called after the swimming figure. "Come back! It's madness to try to swim. Come back! Come back before it is too late! Please!" Sione kept swimming, without response. Aleki watched Sione swim away, convinced he had simply panicked and was running. "It will look bad," he thought. "It will be a great embarrassment to his family."

Sione vanished over the top of a swell, and Aleki looked down at the boat, which was in a sorry state. Gear floated around, fish had begun to work loose from the bags and the covering tarp and were floating all over the boat. "Ioane," he said, "get the gear in order. Cut some line and see if you can tie stuff to the seats. Lafo you get the fish back in the bags and under the tarp."

The two men did as ordered, moving slowly about the boat as it rolled lazily in the swell. Though swamped, the boat was now steady, and there was no immediate danger of it capsizing. When they finished securing the gear and putting the fish under the tarp, Aleki had them sit down to better trim the boat. Shifting his weight from side to side, and having Lafo and Ioane lean in the same direction, allowed him rock the boat. He hoped to wash the water out on one swing and get the boat to a point where the gunwales were out of the water. Then, they could bail the boat out. They tried and tried, achieving only exhaustion; the swamped, loaded boat refused to rock high enough, continuing to roll lazily, one gunwale always just inches under the water, the boat broadside to the heavy sea. Looking at the sky, Aleki could see another squall would soon hit them. If the wind was as strong as the last one, he knew there would be trouble. Looking out toward the island when they reached the top of a swell, he thought he saw the bobbing gas can a few hundred yards away. Closer to the boat, in the lighter colored waters, near the top of a swell, he knew he saw a large shadow race by and a shiver worked through him. He said nothing to the others. "One shark," he thought. "What's one shark?" When he looked again, he thought he saw two shadows, and these were closer.

"Shark! Shark!" screamed Ioane moments later.

Aleki looked at Ioane, to find him pointing to the opposite side of the boat from where he had seen his own shadows. Then, a dark fin cut the water not ten feet from the boat. This was no shadow; it was ten feet of recognizable Tiger shark. It cruised by the starboard side and then circled to the port.

"Another!" screamed Ioane, pointing to a larger gray shape passing under the boat.

"Lafo get the gaff. Ioane get the killing club and find me the hammer from up front," ordered Aleki. He was frightened, but he was not going to give up. He had not believed many sharks would come. When they did, he sensed he might be wrong about much more. He was determined to fight them off if he had to. He was not just going to throw away all he'd worked for. Yet, in the twenty minutes slipping by since Sione had swum away, he'd seen at least four sharks swimming around the boat in ever tightening circles.

<<>>

The second squall worked its way out of the east, releasing a few drops of rain. The men sat silently, watching the close cruising gray shapes as the ocean returned to sadder colors, the sky went gray, and the wind whipped up, pelting them with heavy rain and sea-spray. Ioane was terrified. The wind and rain made it a labor to breathe, and the spray blew into his eyes, blinding him. He was cold and tired. The sharks cruising around the boat made him feel hopeless. He was too frightened even to pray. Lafo sat on the forward bench watching the sharks cruise by, grabbing at floating gear, and trying to secure it. He understood what was happening and wished he could have left the boat with Sione. Aleki was a leader in his family, and he could not leave him, even if he knew Aleki made mistakes. Leaving would bring dishonor to him and the family, so he stayed, and waited; knowing he would not likely see the sunset.

Filled with water and broadside to the swell, the boat became less stable in the heavy winds and rising chop. It rocked precariously as it rose toward the top of the oncoming swell, and rolled back the other way as it descended. As it did, a shark swam close by the boat, almost brushing the side. It was too much for Ioane, who sat not two feet from it as it passed. Ioane saw the Grim

Reaper, and all the fear he had suppressed, the deep despair, came welling up. He jumped to his feet, screaming madly, fleeing what he could not face; in doing so, only running headlong into Death's outstretched arms. His shifting weight, coupled with the rock of the boat as it moved off the top of the swell, created a sickening slow motion roll. First the starboard gunwale rolled far out of water, and then men, gear, and fish slowly spilled into the sea, leaving the boat capsized, its dull red hull facing the sky.

"Get up!" cried Aleki as he tried to climb onto the capsized bottom. It was a deluge, and difficult to see and breathe. The boat provided only slippery handholds. Aleki made it onto the hull, then he pivoted on his chest and belly to look toward the others. Ioane clung to the gunwale. Lafo was nowhere in sight. "Get up!" called Aleki to Ioane. "Here!" he said extending his hand and helping him onto the boat. "Lafo! Where's Lafo?" he screamed at Ioane.

"Don't know," choked Ioane, who was just glad to be out of the water.

Lafo felt the boat going over, and spilled easily into the water. He found his foot caught in line he had used to tie something to the seat. The roll of the boat carried him under the water. He fought to free his leg. The harder he pulled, the tighter the hold on his ankle became. He came up, gasping for air, in a small air pocket under the hull. It was dim, and he could barely see. Disoriented and unable to stay afloat, he banged his head against the bottom of a thwart a few times, gagged, fought for air, sucked in water and quickly slipped into unconsciousness. His final thoughts, after the panic of survival had slipped away, were to give thanks he would not have to watch as the sharks ate him. By the time Aleki had made it to the top of the boat and helped Ioane climb up, Lafo had already drowned.

<<>>

Dead fish floated to the surface, their white bellies glimmering in the windswept water. There was something else in the water too; the sharks had begun to feed. Aleki and Ioane watched as the shiny underbellies of fish were jerked violently from side to side by the frenzied sharks. Fish by fish, the catch was devoured, the remains slowly sinking into the deep.

A slimy layer of brown weed covered the hull, making it difficult to maintain hold to the bottom of the boat. It was unsteady and constantly about to roll one-way or the other. The two men concentrated on spreading out, balancing on the slick hull and trying not to slide off into the sea. Any thought of righting the boat forgotten in the fear of the sharks.

Aleki called Lafo's name a few time, hearing no response. He gave up as the strain of clinging to the boat wore on him. He was cold and drained; desperately tired, he could only think of holding on. The wind and rain lashed the boat, and sea spray stung their eyes. Yet, they could still see the gray torpedo shapes working among the last of the fish. Suddenly the boat jerked to one side, and then sharply to the other. A shark had hit Lafo's body, which floated underneath, still entangled in line. Then, another sharp roll of the boat caused Ioane to his lose hold and slip, ever so slowly, into the water.

"No!" he screamed as he glided slowly toward the water. "Help me! Ohhh, help me Aleki!" he cried.

Aleki slid toward the bow where Ioane clung to the side, trying frantically to climb back onto the hull,. Before Aleki could reach him, Ioane gave a cry, and disappeared under the water. He came back up almost immediately. Aleki could see a shark had hit one of his legs, ripping open a large wound.

"Oh Aleki! Aleki help me! Please!" pleaded Ioane.

Aleki slowly reached for Ioane, making sure he would not also slip into the water. He grabbed Ioane by the hand. "Hold tight! I'll pull you up," he called to Ioane. He edged back along the hull, pulling him up slowly. Suddenly, Ioane jerked again and slipped back into the water, almost pulling Aleki off the slippery hull. Ioane was hysterical now, screaming in panic and fear and pleading with Aleki to help him out of the water. Aleki tried again, managing to pull Ioane onto the hull. Ioane's legs were bleeding badly. He had a ragged wound on his right foot, and another on his left calf; large jagged gashes, both bleeding freely. Ioane whimpered and cried hysterically. Aleki tried to calm him. It did no good. The boat rolled radically again as a shark hit Lafo's suspended body, and Ioane, falling into shock and unable to move his legs, simply slipped headfirst off the opposite side of the overturned boat.

Aleki saw the shark before Ioane. He lay along the spine of the boat, staring as it came slowly along the surface toward Ioane. Ioane did not see it until it brushed by him. Turning his head, he saw the shark, screamed, and then

24

fought wildly to climb back on the boat. The shark rolled abruptly and shot toward him, seizing his left shoulder in its jaws. Its eye rolled out of the water, it stared blankly at Aleki for a frozen instant, then it thrashed and disappeared. Ioane was left floating in dark bloody water, his left side a jagged wound. The shock of the attack took everything from Ioane, the loss of blood acting as a sedative. He floated there briefly, staring at Aleki, trying to say something. It never reached his lips, and he sank slowly into the depths.

When the squall ended, and the sun reappeared, Aleki lay on the top of the boat exhausted. Then, suddenly, the boat jerked and abruptly rolled again. He almost lost his hold as he slid along the hull. His eye caught movement toward the bow. He looked forward and screamed madly, staring in disbelief at Lafo's head bobbing just under the water, his face staring toward Aleki. Then, in the undulations of the swell, Lafo slowly stretched out his right arm and rolled his head from side to side. Aleki knew Lafo was pointing an accusing finger at him and shaking his head in sadness at Aleki's failures.

It was too much for Aleki. In a matter of minutes he had lost his boat. Sione had abandoned him. He had seen Ioane killed by sharks. Now Lafo, a loyal member of his family, had come from the dead to accuse him of responsibility for it all. He lay there, talking to the dead man, pleading with him to understand how sorry he was for it all, how he did not mean for it to happen this way.

"Lafo!" called Aleki. "Get up here! When the squall is past, we will right the boat. Don't worry about the sharks. It is going to be all right." His words made no difference to Lafo, his head just kept moving from side to side as the swells ran past the boat. When Aleki could bear the accusing stare no longer, he turned around, and moved toward the stern, moaning and weeping, trying not to look at Lafo.

Lafo's body continued to attract sharks, and they circled the boat hitting the corpse, or what remained of it, for hours. Even when the last vestiges of the body were torn from under the boat, some persistent individuals continued to circle the overturned hull. Perhaps the sharks sensed Aleki was lying just out of reach, or they stayed near what was the floating marker of a good feed. Hour by hour, Aleki went increasingly mad, and it did not matter much to him why they were there. He only knew he must stay on the hull, and he clung to it with perseverance far beyond normal strength.

When Sione fell into the water, he reached out for the gas can and without looking back toward the boat, started kicking toward the distant hazy blue mountains lying far off to the south. He had no delusions about reaching shore; he simply knew he would not die in the boat. So, he swam away. He ignored Aleki's calls, knowing it was useless to argue and hoping to get as far away from the bloody wreck as quickly as possible. Then, just minutes after he had left the boat, his muscles tightened as he saw a long brown shadow flash by in the light blue sheen of a passing swell. They had come, as he knew they would. His only hope was the scent of the fish blood would allow him to hide in the ocean.

He swam hard, pushing the gas can in front of him, not getting far before exhaustion demanded he rest. Hugging the can, he drifted in the swell, waiting for his strength to return. On one rise and fall, coincidence brought him to the top of the swell as the boat was still rising on another. He found he was looking toward the boat, which was a few hundred yards away. He could make out the men in the boat, and conditions appeared unchanged. He was not certain, he thought he also saw the outline of a shark fin at the top of a swell. Before he could make sure, he was riding down and into another valley of water, and the boat was gone. Waiting, he slid to the bottom of the swell and then rode the opposing incline. At the crest he looked for the boat, and saw only empty ocean.

"If he gets rid of the fish and stays calm, Aleki might still make it," he thought. He pushed the can in front of him and started kicking toward the island. The intermittent squalls were a relief from the hot sun and offered him a slight, frustrating opportunity, to get some fresh water. The experiences of the day had sapped him, and he floated almost as much as he swam. He had tied a big loop of rope through the handle of the can and pulled it over his arms. It allowed him to hang on to the can and drift off to sleep without great danger of drowning.

Hours passed. It grew dark and chilly. Fits of shivering overcame him, and if it had not been for the rope he would have lost hold of the can and simply slipped under the swell. The night was long, and he was swimming before first light, surprised at his condition, as he had not expected to be alive. His hands and feet were puckered and white, his lips were cracked, and his eyes burned. He had strength, and as soon as the sun showed its false dawn, he was kicking toward the south. Progress was slow, and what a boat could do in hours, he realized would take him days. The current was slowly sweeping him along, and he could make out the outline of mountains far to the west of his village. He knew if it took too long to reach shore, he would miss the island. The sweet air of the morning felt good in his lungs, and he released these concerns as he paced his kicks to a stroke he felt he could continue for hours.

In the late afternoon Sione had a visitor. He could not tell what it was. The dark shape circled him, keeping its distance. Suddenly it moved toward him, shying away as he beat on the can with the palm of his hand. A moment later, it was gone. The adrenalin rush robbed him of his small reserve of strength and his progress slowed. By evening he held on to the can, drifting mostly, and falling asleep between periods of kicking and fits of shivers. He could see the lights on shore and knew if he made it through the night it was possible he would see his wife and children; it kept him fighting.

The next morning found him slipping in and out of consciousness; his lips badly cracked, his tongue feeling like a large rag stuffed into his throat, kept threatening to gag him. His eyes burned and were almost swollen shut. A painful sore had developed under his arm where the rope had worn a track in his flesh as the can bobbed in the swell. His confused thoughts were almost entirely about water; showers under a flowing pipe, rivers, and great gulps of clear, shiny water going down his throat in magical bursts. He fought to convince his body it was only by continued kicking he could gain these prizes. One kick followed the next, one breath gave him the resolve to take another. It was a battle of moments; and the agony was constant, he hid in between the intervals of pain.

He reached the outer reef in the late morning and floated there, just beyond the combers, wondering what to do. He knew the waves and the reef would beat him up badly if he just pushed in. He drifted toward a small channel offering a precarious passage into the lagoon, and after an extraordinary fight, he managed to ride the can over the coral heads and onto the top of the massive reef wall. He nearly drown on two occasions as the water became shallow, and huge waves pounded in on him. The floating can caught in the surge of the breakers, dragged him over the sharp coral, ripping deep cuts and scratches along his body. His knees and his feet were severely gashed, and he found it impossible to stand. He was forced to make a long, agonizing crawl across the reef. He collapsed in the shallows on the inner side of the reef, watching as threads of blood whirled around him in the light currents.

An hour later, his feeble waves and weak calls caught the notice of fisherman in a small outrigger. He crawled into the canoe and collapsed as he was paddled the long distance to shore. It was there he found the magical drink of cool drink of water he had long been promising himself.

<>>

Sione's rescue prompted the government to launch an air-sea search for the fishing boat, which had already been reported overdue. Based on information from Sione and common knowledge about currents and drift, a wreck was sighted within twenty-four hours. The pilot of the one engine plane found what appeared to be a boat, made several low passes. Neither he nor his spotter could see any signs of life on, or around, the half-submerged wreck.

They could not be certain the debris they saw was Aleki's boat. They spotted nothing else along the drift path resembling a boat.

On their return, and after official discussions, it was decided 'not to attempt locating the wreck by motor vessel'. The official record simply stated, 'Three men lost at sea in a twenty-four foot fishing boat, one survivor washed ashore.'

Night Fishing

"So, Sa'aga, can you tell us the tale about fishing with Tomas and his son?" asked Sauaso, with a raised eyebrow to the others sitting on the mats. "Tell us about that night," he continued in a soothing voice as he cued Lalo to pour Sa'aga another glass of Steinlager *For Export Only* Lager.

There were five men sitting in the small back fale of Sauaso's family compound. It was a secluded place where the sea breezes blew the mosquitoes away, sitting far from the prying eyes of the women of his family and others who might cluck and chick their cheeks loudly about men drinking on a Saturday afternoon.

His crew was thirsty and tired. A morning of fishing had baked them nut-brown. The salt breezes had crusted their eyelids and turned their eyes red. They had fished since before dawn, managed a good catch, come home, cleaned the gear, showered quickly, and then piled into Sauaso's truck to sell the catch in the villages along the road toward town. Now, in mid-afternoon on a day beginning hours before dawn, they were done, and it was Sauaso's responsibility to relax his crew, to get them moderately drunk and happy. He needed these four scaly turtles again on Monday. Sauaso raised an eyebrow as he smiled

31

at Sa'aga, signaling Lalo to fill the glass and urged Sa'aga to tell one of the renowned fishing stories of the district. It was a story they had all heard before, had all heard Sa'aga tell before. It was a tale never losing its ability to send a chill down the back. It was a fine story with which to suck down a beer and feel the cool breezes rush over salt chafed and sunburned skin. It was a good tale to tell after you had come home and could look out on the sea from the comfort of a small earthbound fale.

Sa'aga saw Lalo pouring the beer before he heard the question. He was thirsty, and the first few glasses had been poured slowly. He wanted this one, gratefully anticipated the cool bitterness, of it slipping down his throat, and yearned for the soft shudder that would spread from his shoulder blades. Sauaso let Sa'aga eye the beer and drink a long deep swig. He raised an eyebrow, and Lalo filled the glass again, almost before it hit the mat. Sa'aga tossed back another deep gulp, shuddered and looked at Sauaso almost uncomprehendingly.

At first he was a bit embarrassed at his lack of courtesy to the others. Then, Sauaso's request slipped slowly out of his subconscious, and he was thankful for the extra few glasses of bitter brew. He felt a slight shudder of fear and remembrance pass over him rather than the cool alcohol shiver he had been expecting again. The hair rose on his arms and the back of his neck.

He looked at Sauaso and then slowly at the others who sat calmly awaiting his decision. Taking another long gulp of brew, he let out a long breath and began his tale.

<><>

"I used to fish with Tomas when I was younger. He was the only man in the village who would take a young man like me go out," he said pointing at his mangled legs. "It wasn't because he was European, or he felt sorry for me. He never made it easy on me. I worked as hard fishing then as I do now," he added proudly. "Tomas, he said I was a good worker and better than the other boys, and he gave me a fair share. So I was happy working with him.

First, we had an ali'a with a twenty horse Johnson. It was always either too wet and damn cold, or blistering hot. I hated that double-hulled demon! We fished well, and Tomas managed to save enough money from the catches to buy a new Fisheries diesel. A big boat, almost thirty feet, with high gunnels to kept it dry and allow you to get out of the wind if you got cold. It was better than the ali'a. Big enough for five men and gear. Less than we get in Sauaso's whaleboat. The diesel had a narrower beam which allowed it to move better through the chop. Despite its V bottom it rolled in a swell if it wasn't up to speed. Not a boat Ropati would like," he said smiling at one of the men across the mat.

Ropati giggled, and the others laughed and kidded him for his well-known tendency to seasickness, even in the slightest swell.

Sauaso nodded and passed the green Gray's tobacco box. Lalo poured another round

Sa'aga rolled a cigarette looking into the cardboard box of stringy soft brown tobacco as if he was seeing the threads of his memories.

"He was a good man," he said to his friends, "and a real fisherman." He passed the box of tobacco as the others nodded in silent agreement. Then he continued.

"We fished for six months and everything was good. The engine was reliable. The boat held together well. We went out three or four days a week. It was mostly bottom fishing. Sometimes we chased the schools of aku. The boat was a bit slow to go after the schools. We mostly went bottom fishing at night, far out near the triple humps," he said referring to a place they all knew.

"Tomas liked the humps. He liked *filoa*, spotcheek emperor, because they sold well, and we could catch many out there. The boat rolled badly in the swells coming up over the humps, so we always had trouble keeping the boat crewed. We would get fellows to join us for a few weeks, and then after they had a pocket full of money, they would suddenly say it made them too sick to go there all the time. We were always looking for crew. Tomas liked the humps and said he would find some hard cases someday, who could put up with the rock and roll of the boat."

"Well, like I said, we did well for six months. Then his oldest son asked if he could join us. The kid was a bit young, close to fourteen, He was big and he could work. Tomas told me he did not want to take him out. On weekends it was always a tough to get a full crew together so he relented. You know the boy turned out to be a real fisherman. He could hook 'em. I would have to help occasionally on the bigger fish. He caught more than his share. The boy only had one problem. He thought he knew all the answers. He wouldn't always listen to Tomas, or even me. A strange fourteen year old don't you think?" he said, smiling at the others.

34

Sa'aga looked around at the faces, which were filled with hidden anticipation, and then at his ever so full glass. He took a long drink, a hit of his Gray's and let out a long smoky breath, peering into its fog as if it could tell his fortune. The time had come.

"One Saturday night when the moon rose like a giant orange, and the sea was as silvery smooth as the beach at low tide, we went out to the humps. It was slow. You know, good weather, bad fishing. Get a night when you cannot hold down your guts, and the fish are jumping into the boat. Well it was a perfect night. We sat there bouncing our weights off the bottom for an hour, and nothing. The boy was in the bow, I was amidships, and Tomas was fishing off the stern.

We talked for a while, and dozed a bit as the time crept by. The boy was laying on the forward seat. You know, we were all tired, and I didn't take much notice. We were not catching anything. I should have noticed! I had warned him a few times about it. I should have looked to make sure. I didn't," he said condemning himself sadly to the others.

The others stared back at him silently, sympathy showing in their eyes and on their faces. Each man already knew what it was Sa'aga had not done, yet each awaited his revelation.

"The boy had looped the line around his wrist!" Sa'aga exclaimed. "Looped it and was pulling on it occasionally as the boat rolled lightly. You couldn't see it because his arm was in the bilge! Anyway, along about three hours, and the kid got a bite. No, it was not a bite, it was an awesome yank, and it half pulled him out of the boat. One second he was lying on the seat, and the next, he was half in the water! He managed to pull himself back into the boat, and we looked at each other for an instant. He was too scared to even scream. In the moonlight, I could see his eyes, and they told me he feared what was going to happen. He tried desperately to get the line off his wrist, but could not, and then it happened. Before I could even move from my seat, his arm jerked a bit and went right over the side. His hand reel started to jump around like a chicken with no head. I got to the line, but I could not do anything with it. It was moving out so fast I almost couldn't touch it. In desperation, I just grabbed it and wrapped some of it around an oarlock. That's where I got this," he said holding up his right hand, the little finger missing two joints. "It went right through and it was moving so fast it damn near cauterized the end. I didn't bleed much, at least not that I could tell later."

"Tomas had moved faster than I. He was farther back in the boat. When he reached me I had the line tied off. We grabbed it together and tried to pull. It was like steel cable it was so tight. We couldn't pull anything in! Then Tomas yells for me to cut the anchor rope. 'We'll move with it and pull the line up!' he screamed. It took me less than a minute to find a knife and hack the anchor rope. All the time, Tomas is pulling on the kid's line, and it's turning the palms of his hands into bloody meat. We were getting nowhere.

"The boat is moving through the water, and the line is still almost impossible to pull in. We are screaming at each other, still pulling on the line. It was obvious we are not going to pull the boy up and there is no telling how deep he is. Then Tomas yells at me for the knife. I hand it to him, and with only a word or two, he puts the knife in his teeth, and dives down the line."

36

Sa'aga stopped and stared at his mates, then continued "And you know," he said looking again at the men around him. "I have never been so alone in all my life, those few seconds after Tomas went into the water. One minute it was chaos, and the next it was dead quiet. The only sound, the eerie rush of the boat through the water. I sat there gazing over the side. I could not cut the line. It was their path back. I couldn't pull on it. My hand hurt so bad I could barely grab anything. I just sat there, hoping to see them come out of the water.

"It wasn't over a minute or two, though it seemed like an hour, when the boat just stopped rushing through the water. I reached for the line and pulled it up, pulled faster and then just stopped; it was slack. I looked out over the side, expecting to see them. At least Tomas. Nothing happened. No one came up! Not even Tomas. Nothing! I sat there staring out over the water, hoping, praying for some sign they were alive. all I saw was a glassy sea. Then after I had given up on seeing them again, I hear something knock the boat. At first I think it's Tomas, and I lean over, looking to give him a hand.

"It wasn't Tomas. No, I don't know what it was. The moon only shimmered off parts of it. It was big though, and it came to tell me it knew where Tomas and the boy were. It kept knocking the boat, not violently, mind you. It was playing with it, playing with me. Then my line went taut and began pulling the boat. I'd forgotten it, you see. The other lines were still over the side. We'd pulled them off the bottom, and tied them off. I found the ax we had, and I just whacked away at the line until I cut it. Then, before I could get to the stern, it did the same with Tomas' line! When I got Tomas' cut, it came back and started knocking the boat again."

Sa'aga sat there shaking his head. Looking wide-eyed at the others who sat drinking their beers and smoking their hand rolled cigarettes with quiet deliberation.

"It went on for hours. Hours! You see I didn't know much about the diesel. Tomas had always run it. And the night was dark, despite the moon, and I couldn't see much," his voice trailed off. "When I moved, it would knock the boat harder. I just sat there, too scared to even move!"

He took a long pull on his beer and relit his Gray's, aware the difficult part of the story was told. "Around dawn it just went away," he continued. "Maybe it tired. I don't know. I never knew what it was. Never did see it well."

"In the morning light I could see the engine better, and I got it started and headed the boat back. Tomas's family went crazy when they heard the story. Some of you saw that sad scene.

"Me? I got off the boat and swore I would never go out again. Well I guess it was two month before I was fishing again. Man with my legs can't grow Taro!" he laughed. "I'm bound to the sea! You know, I never like to go back to those damn humps! No, all the filoa in the ocean cannot make the humps attract me! That fellow out there, he can go play 'knock knock' with someone else!" He chuckled to the group.

Sauaso and the others quietly nodded their agreement. Sauaso moved his finger in a small arc, and Lalo poured another round for the thirsty men. Another few stories, thought Sauaso, then some food, and the boys can go home and sleep or bother their wives.

"Reminds me of the time I speared a giant octopus and nearly drown. Still have these," he said pointing at the large circular welts across his chest. He took a long swig of beer, setting the glass on the mat.

Lalo moved to refill it with great care.

Fishermen

I t was a clear and beautiful morning, filled with soft mountain breezes lightly swaying the coconut fronds and bringing a slight chill to the air. The village was already awake as the sun sent daggers of orange fire across the eastern sky. Families had gathered in the small fale along the beach of the bay. Quick meals of hot sweet cocoa scented with lime leaves and thick with bits of freshly roasted beans and large ship's biscuits, were eaten in haste as people prepared for the morning's work.

Fa'afetai walked slowly toward the sea, feeling the light breezes on his bare legs as he stared out over the bay. The waves played easily over the coral buttresses near the point, and the glassy shimmer of the distant ocean spoke of a day of little chop and ideal fishing. He squatted on his haunches and studied the subtleties of the water as it shimmered like an octopus, following the slow transition of the sky from silver to pale blue. He breathed deeply occasionally, filling his lungs with the pleasantly damp air whispering past him and watched the breezes dancing out onto the surface of the bay.

It was a morning all a morning could ever be. Even the flies appeared overcome by the beauty and wandered slowly over damp surfaces, drunk on the dew left by the quiet night. High on the mountain, across the bay, the trees suddenly turned a golden green, almost bronzed by the first light of the sun. Slowly, the golden glow worked its way down the steep cliffs, burning away the light mists and subtly bringing on the verdant green chaos of day. He sat there at sunrise, day after day, for years, watching. There was always something to learn about the dawn, always a detail revealed, a new appreciation, a change from the day before. He always learned something about the life he lived and the day to come. Today as he studied the long stretch of beach, he noticed a coconut tree had fallen in the night. It lay across the beach, its fronds washed by the rippling tide, roots upturned, its trunk pointing toward a coral cove at the edge of the reef; a favorite fishing spot. He knew the tree, had climbed it as boy, run out along its narrowing trunk and dropped into the shallow surf. Now it lay across the sands, overcome by the tides.

An omen? Perhaps. Fa'afetai studied the tree, and he slowly let his eyes follow the pointing trunk to the white foam washing the edge of the underwater cove. It was a calm, blue sea he saw. In his mind he had a vision of a fairyland of coral castles, valleys, and caverns of stone. It was the world beneath the waves, the land of the hunt, where he could fly like a gull through the water.

The morning's adventure lay before him, even as the sun's rays marched down the beach like a band of warriors setting the world ablaze. When they struck him with their hot flares, he rose from his seat and walked slowly toward home to get his spear, goggles and fins.

"Fa'afetai, a good morning to you, honored chief," called a man in his mid-thirties, walking slowly from a fale near his own. "I trust you found a good beginning to this day",

42

he continued. "And it will bring us a greater appreciation of our short and happy lives," he said with a soft smile.

"Ho, Samuelu! Greetings, my most favored spokesman. Yes, it is a beautiful morning. May we thank the Good Lord. The start of a fine day and, if blessed, one upon which we will be most fortunate," laughed Fa'afetai. "See the old coconut tree that fell into the sea last night?" he asked, gesturing to the far beach. "It points toward the outer cove. The seas are mild, and the heat of this early morning says the sea breezes will not pick up until late in the day. So good friend, today it is the spear. The aku will wait. Besides, the early heat does not speak well for a man's good luck on the deep blue swells of yonder ocean. Get your dive gear and your canoe, and off we will go to find our fortune!"

The men laughed at their unnecessary formality, for they had known each other since the times when the sea had been, the smallest of waves brushing the sands of this same beach. A time when they had danced at its edges with fairies only they could see and been drawn to a world playing a siren's song which made them fishermen. Today, as they had done for years, they prepared to go out together into the sea they loved, respected and yet, always feared.

They were in the water quickly. Their out-rigger canoes were sleek and beautifully cared for and glided over the bay with the lightest of strokes. Each canoe was custom-built. Together the men had sought the trees for the hulls, wandering for months in the uplands before finding just the right ones. Then under a shed between their fale, they had hollowed out the trunks with adzes and chisels. Built together, they were, never-the-less, as different as the trees from which they were hued, and the men who would sit in them. The canoes were unique creations of beauty and deep knowledge. Fa'afetai's was longer, deeper and wider, because of his added weight. While Samuelu had made the outrigger longer in relation to the hull, to counter his preference for paddling on the outer side. They were the fastest canoes on the coast and proved it in many celebration day races.

They reached the cove and tied their canoes to coral heads in the shallow waters of a tidal channel. Then, fixing their gear; handmade goggles, spears with Hawaiian slings, and duck feet—gifts from departing Peace Corps Volunteers—they slipped into the large sunken valley in the underwater world of the cove. The water was cool on their skin, and clear, the bottom, at seventy feet, unclouded and seemingly close. Fish floated all about them like exotic birds. Some basked in the sunny waters unmoving, while others danced like hummingbirds and butterflies from coral flower to coral flower.

At the open edge of the bowl they saw large gray clouds of coral sand, evacuated by a small school of giant parrotfish, which dashed off when the men dropped into the water. On the bottom, in a meadow of sand, they could make out a giant ray, lying motionless and almost invisible. The good fishing was along the walls of the cove, where the coral flowed like soft putty, making canyons and caverns where the choicest of fish hid.

The men started working the inner curve of the bowl. They knew the area like the paths of their village. They would drop down along the wall and work their way along the long crevices eventually closing into caverns. There, up in the darkest places, lurked the tasty red squirrel and soldier fish; fish too quick for most to spear. Not too quick for either Fa'afetai or Samuelu.

44

Each dive lasted about two minutes, and each one resulted in a catch. These they strung on a coconut frond fiber attached to their waists; and when they had a half-dozen or so each, they would swim back to the boats to unload their catch and grab another tether.

"The water is beautiful today, eh Fa'afetai," said Samuelu as they clung to the sides of their canoes. "I enjoy it most when it is like this—clear and cool. I could stay out here forever."

"Samele would not appreciate a fish for a husband," Fa'afetai laughed. "Yes, I sometimes wish I was born a turtle, with a life where I could always glide along the edges of these canyons and coves."

"You know the aku are the fish to chase, and the hunt is always exciting; but it is only when we spearfish I feel the cool calculation of the hunt," confided Samuelu.

"It is the water," nodded Fa'afetai. "It cleanses you. The coolness of the ocean seeps into your pores and brings a soft peace to your soul. When we aku fish, we fight the sun and the sea. We wear broad hats and shirts, and still, the sun's fire heats our brains and makes us mad, I think. The madness is part of the reason for going out; to drench oneself in the blood lust of the chase. No better way to feel like a man, a predator, than to chase the aku. Yet here, in the cove, it is quiet, swift, and clean. We must seek a fish, aim, and let fly our spear. Except for a bit of wriggling and biting the head, it is complete. The skill is difficult to learn, the kill is direct and not so steeped in the traditions of the hunt."

"I am of the water," said Samuelu, dipping his head in the water to cool it from the heat of the sun. "I love the aku," he continued as he resurfaced, "days like this bring me peace of mind. I am always happy when you choose the spear rather than the pole. Yes, it is the coolness seeping into me, and when I go home—well, Samele says I am a softer and gentler lover in the night. She teases me sometimes about the aku chase. When we leave in the morning she often complains quietly about it meaning we will make love until dawn. It is true. I am on fire when we come home late in the afternoon, the canoe full of blood, the smell of the fish, and the salt caked on my lips. I can see why the men toward town drink so much after chasing the schools. For me," he laughed, "I prefer my wife's cure for the madness of the day."

"Yes," said Fa'afetai. "I understand."

The men floated in the sea, taking an occasional drink of water, while they hid in the shade of the canoe hulls.

"Well, let's get back to it," suggested Fa'afetai ending the brief rest. He reached into his canoe and took a final gulp of water from the glass jug he had tucked under the foredeck.

"Yes. Let's split up this time. I'll head toward the point, and you can work the edge toward the bay," suggested Samuelu.

"As you wish."

The men swam in different directions along the edge of the sunken cove. They would dive in unison, finding fish and spearing them. Then they would come to the surface and with subconscious thought, check to see the other's head as he too, came to the surface. It went on like this for an hour. Occasionally they would make the easy swim back to the boats where they would drop their catch, take a drink, and talk softly as they floated, heads bobbing in the narrowing shadows of the outrigger hulls.

On one dive, Fa'afetai saw a turtle, a hawksbill, drifting quietly along the bottom toward the bay. He loved the turtle, The hawksbill was his aumakua, his spirit of protection in the sea. He dove down toward it, swimming deep, perhaps sixty feet. The turtle saw him coming, swam on undisturbed. His ears aching and his lungs burning, Fa'afetai reached out and stroked the turtle's shell, his hand brushing a back fin. The turtle cocked its head and looked at him for a peaceful moment, and then, in one powerful stroke of its fins, jetted off into the blue-gray distance.

Fa'afetai was elated. To touch a turtle was, for him, a wonder of life. It had only happened twice before. He was so pleased he almost forgot the pain in his ears and the aching of his lungs. As he turned and headed toward the surface, a great surge of adrenalin pumped through his body. It was not for touching the turtle. An instant after a great gray-brown shape charged passed him. It was so quick he could not tell what it was, only it was large, and it had a mouth full of teeth.

As the sweet air filled his lungs he swam quickly to the edge of the bowl, hoping the shallower waters of the reef would offer some protection. Then he looked off toward the point where Samuelu was diving, ready to warn his friend of the danger. He saw nothing. He looked out toward the ocean and then slowly back toward the boats. He could not see his companion's outline against the swell. He felt deep concern and gazed desperately at the last place he had seen Samuelu. Fa'afetai's hopes could not bring his friend to the surface. Long after Samuelu should have come up to breathe, Fa'afetai swam cautiously along the rim of the cove, toward where his friend had been diving.

The view of the bottom was clear, and the sides of the walls revealed only dancing and dipping brightly colored fish. Where he should have found Samuelu, he found nothing. He swam toward the point, far beyond where he knew Samuelu had been and saw only fish; no spear, no goggles, or fins, no Samuelu. He became exhausted, was finished searching, and made his way slowly back to the boats. He climbed into his canoe and lay on the bottom shivering uncontrollably, the sun searing his flesh as the breezes chilled him. Occasionally he would look toward the point. He had long realized there was no sense. As far as the sea was concerned, Samuelu had never existed. He was gone, without a trace.

Fa'afetai lay in the bottom of the canoe. Tears would not come. Perhaps it was the shock, or acceptance of what he and Samuelu knew was the unavoidable fact in a fisherman's life; there may be a day when you just did not paddle home. Today was Samuelu's day, the day he was lost to the sea.

Fa'afetai shook his head sadly and a chill passed through him. Had it not been just minutes ago his friend had wished to dive forever? "Well," he whispered to the ocean, "you have your wish my friend, and may you be always happy with it. As for me, I will tell your wife you are where you longed to be, perhaps sooner than you expected. You are there all the same. Someday, we will fish together again. I am sure." Then, he dove down, untied the canoes, and started the long lonely paddle back to the village, which would tonight echo with the mournful cries of women and children. Later, deep in the night, he would whisper to his wife of the hawksbill turtle

48

he had touched and the terrible loss he felt on this fine and beautiful day.

Boat Anchor

S ale sat back against a support pole of the fale, took a long drag on the Grey's he had just rolled, and moaned loudly, letting the smoke escape slowly from his lungs. "Thanks be to those who cooked this wonderful meal," he said as he winked at Sisifo and Sala, his wife and eldest daughter. He smiled at his cousin, who lay heavy on the mats like a collection of half-filled bags of copra.

"It is good to have you here Filo," he said. "It is almost a year since you have come home. We like having you with us again. It is time we had the opportunity to show our thanks for all your help with the boys," he added, alluding to Filo's boarding of his two older sons in town during the school year.

"Think nothing of it Sale," said Filo, waving his hand depreciatingly in the air from his prone position on the mats. "I'm happy to do it. It is family. We are all family, Eh?" he concluded waving his hands again and giggling softly.

"Well I am in your debt cousin, and I thank you all the same."

"It is fine being here," said Filo as he rolled onto his large stomach, splaying out his legs like stabilizers, and making

51

himself a cigarette from the green Grey's Tobacco tin Sale slid to him across the mats. "Sometimes I think about quitting that damn job in town, coming back home, perhaps starting a small plantation. Who knows? Maybe even doing some fishing. I imagine I could make good money planting taro and banana. The price of fish is so high in town anyone could make much money fishing!"

"The price of fish is high enough here in the village to make a fisherman rich," added Sale lazily as he took another drag on his cigarette. "You need a boat and a motor to fish for money, and it is only old Fagaese and Tupua who have them," he added, shaking his head sadly as he exhaled the rest of the smoke.

"The high chief and the pastor!" exclaimed Filo, shaking his head and sucking his cheek against his teeth and making a chicking sound in sympathy. "Always the same. Always the politicians and the pastors. They always have a lock on the opportunity. Doesn't it make you sick Sale?"

Sale looked at his cousin cautiously. He was uncomfortable with such talk. "No," he said softly. "Why should it make me sick? It's just the way it is."

"Don't you wish it were different? Don't you wish you had a chance to make lots money? Be a big man?"

"I don't know. I never thought about it," said Sale honestly. "My family, my work; the days are full. I am happy. The boys do well, and my daughters do even better. Sisifo still smiles for me. What more can a man of my age ask?"

"More money!" exclaimed Filo. "Wouldn't you like to have more money? Build a European house? Own a new truck?" asked Filo, becoming animated.

"I like the fale. My great-grandfather built this house. It feels like family. My father made this mark on the post when he was three," he said with a smile, pointing at a notch on the dark hand rubbed support post he was sitting against. "My truck runs fine. I paid for it two years ago." Sale gazed at his cousin blankly, wondering what he wanted, dreading what he was about to be bound to, and puzzled why Filo danced around it so. "Must be the way they act in town," he thought. He smiled inwardly at his cousin, amazed at his town ways. "And what would I have to do to be able to afford a European house," he asked rhetorically, reluctantly wanting Filo to get to the point of this uncomfortable conversation.

"Well, if you owned a boat, you could go fishing and sell the extra fish in the village. Maybe, even truck the rest to town! You would be rich fast, no doubt! And you could build a European style fale!"

"Filo, I don't own a motor. I don't even own a boat, let alone know how to use either of them. I don't have money for either. You are right; if I had them I guess I could make money."

"Well! I know how we can get them!" exclaimed Filo with an excited smile lighting up his face, and announcing the reason for his visit.

Sale sat staring at his cousin, saying nothing, hoping if he just became inert and looked outside, perhaps Filo would forget what he was saying. Hoping Filo would pass out as he always did, from all the food he stuffed into his gut at evening meal. Hoping the oozy feeling in his own stomach would go away. Hoping the nightmare vision of bobbing around endlessly in a small boat would fade from his mind. His hopes were in vain. He sat there watching light breezes sway the giant leaves of the breadfruit tree just outside the fale until the uneasiness in his gut threatened to take his dinner. Shuddering lightly he looked back at Filo, who was still all smiles. "At least ten of them!" thought Sale. Filo had a big one on his face, and the two meaty ones on his neck. There was a smile inside each arm. He could see a few half-hidden smiles on Filo's enormous belly as they peeked out through the opening in the lava-lava he had draped over his shoulders. Sale thought he could even see a few on Filo's feet. "He's all smiles," he complained silently, "and I want to cry!" He smiled a small, painful, and reluctant smile of his own back at Filo.

"It will be easy Sale!" said Filo triumphantly. I have a friend who will help us. He works for the Development Bank. We can get a loan! And I can get us a boat and motor through the Agriculture Department where I work. It will all be quite simple."

"Filo, if it is so simple, why do you need me? Your thoughtfulness is greatly appreciated, yet certainly not necessary." said Sale trying to make one final escape from the unavoidable reality of the boat and motor. Filo ignored Sale's graciousness and sped on.

"These loans, boats, and the motors, are only for villagers. Town people, and particularly Bank and Agriculture Department employees, cannot receive them. No. If you applied, you would get one for sure!"

"I'm not a fisherman, why would I get one?" asked Sale, not wanting to know.

"Because I manage the list of those who are approved for a boat and motor, explained Filo with a broad smile, and my friend does the same for development loans at the bank. I just need you to apply. You apply and I will approve the boat and the motor! And my friend will see to the approval of the loan for the boat and motor!"

"Filo, my dear cousin, if I get the loan, doesn't it mean I must then repay the loan for the boat and motor?"

"Don't worry! We will be rich men! The boat and the motor will allow us to catch plenty fish! Paying the loan will be easy."

"I don't know. I have my plantation. It keeps me busy. I'm not much of a fisherman you know. I get seasick easily. They say it is not good fishing here. I don't think I own any hooks. Don't eat much fish anyway. Never did like the water. Ummmm," he said, running out of excuses.

"Sale! Sale! Please! Sale for me? It will be a grand adventure. Do this for me so I can come home. Please!" whined Filo in an all too familiar tone of voice.

And Sale did as he always knew he would, as he always did from the time when they had been young boys hauling coconuts home from the plantation after school and Filo wanted to go play in the sea when there was work to do. He said, "Sure cousin," and, as in all the other instances, he found himself staring into the stern face of his father, having no excuse for the utter stupidity he had just committed, hearing his father sucking his cheek slowly against his teeth, it making a chicking sound, and watching the old man shake his slightly bowed head in painful sadness. It was always the way when he let Filo talk him into something stupid. He could never refuse his cousin's pleading requests. Nothing had changed, except his father was gone, and now he looked up to find Sisifo gazing at him in shocked surprise, and with the same sad look his father had always had on his face at times like this.

<<>>

In a few short months, the boat, the motor, and a large and heavy packet full of papers declaring him the borrower of a large amount of money and the operator of a boat and motor, were all Sale's. He, Filo, and Setuloa, another cousin, brought the boat along the coast to the village with only minor problems. It was a voyage of great smiles over a sea of wonderful expectations. Even Sale started to believe his future was bright. Certainly, the beer they had on board did much to soothe his seasickness and add to the euphoria of the trip. They caught some fish as they trolled down the coast and when they arrived home, the village greeted them like heroes returning from war.

The crowd waited on the shore, and the village minister was there to lead prayers of thanksgiving and say a blessing for the success of the boat and safety of the men. He received the first and best of the catch from the trip from town. The high chief of the village was also present. After much formality, many speeches, and a large gift of fish to the High Chief, he wished Sale and his family good luck, confirming his permission for the venture; permission Sale had sought and received long before he went to town to sign papers. Even Sisifo had a smile for him, the first since his involvement in Filo's newest scheme. The evening meal was a celebration, and there was much talk of the wonders of the boat and the great voyage of bringing it all the way from town.

56

After dinner there was some discussion of when they would go fishing. Sale suggested they wait a few days to get a feel for all the gear and equipment. Filo just shook his head and said "Tomorrow! The sooner we go out the faster we can make money!" Reluctantly, Sale consented and they turned in early, ready to begin their first fishing trip in the morning.

Dawn was still an hour away when Sale and Setuloa finished loading the last of the gear into the boat. They had more line and fishing gear than Sale had ever seen in one place, and with the water jugs, food baskets, and gas can, it made for a crowded boat. The day looked calm, and he hoped they would not go too far, nor be away too long. Filo was still asleep when he came back up to the house. Sisifo was up, and she eyed him cautiously, saying nothing. She did not approve of Filo or his many schemes, This one worried her more than the others. She showed it through her cool silence. After showering, Sale sat down for breakfast and called across the open room to waken Filo. He asked his youngest daughter to bring a large cup of sweetened tea for her uncle Filo.

"It's a beautiful day Filo. We should have some good fishing."

Filo looked across the room, let out a low moan, and shook his head after his first drink of steaming tea. "Too much beer yesterday. The sun and the beer gave me a real headache."

"We are all ready. Setu and I have been up for a few hours. The boat is ready to go. We'll leave after we eat," said Sale, ignoring Filo's foul mood. Filo just stared at him in disgust.

After breakfast they said good-bye to the family and waded out to the boat, which was moored in the shallows of the inner cover. Setuloa was in charge of the engine for the simple reason he was the only one who had ever used an outboard before the trip from town. He was also the one among them who had done much fishing. They felt he would be able to find the fish better. That Setu was one of the slower witted members of the family was not forgotten. Under the circumstances, it was generously overlooked.

"After all," Filo had said, "we are going fishing not opening a store. Setu can find fish, and he can drive the boat. It is enough." Sale had agreed, knowing in matters needing little deep thought, Setu was a good man to have along. Sale was still nervous. All the money tied up in the boat and motor, and he did not know much about it all. It was difficult for him.

They cast off, and Sale waved a silent good-bye to Sisifo and the rest of his family who were gathered on the narrow sandy shore. Then, before he knew it, his attention focused on poling out to deeper water, getting the engine started, and balancing the boat so all three men could sit down amid all the gear. Once seated, they concentrated on the fishing. Thanks to Setu the hand lines were rigged, and they got the lines out just after passing beyond the reef.

They pushed out toward the blue-gray mountains of the neighboring island. The sun rose off to the starboard, and the dark sea became a glistening lake of quicksilver, rippling with red tinted rills as the sky shimmered from black, to purple, toward pink, and then through lighter shades of blue. It was a wonderful sight, and Sale looked at Filo and smiled uneasily.

58

"We're fishing now!" yelled Filo in response, with a big grin on his face. They all giggled at one another nervously.

The boat hadn't gone a fifty yards beyond the cut in the reef when a fish hit one of the lines, and Filo pulled in a small malauli, a jack. Smiles got broader and confidence went up. Thirty minutes later, Sale saw a smudge on the western horizon and pointed it out to Setu. "Birds!" cried Setu as the bow swung westward. The engine whined loudly turning up a light blue ribbon of airy sea and sent strong vibrations through the boat. The men checked their lines, strained to see the birds, and sat there smiling at one another in their excitement.

Ten minutes later, they were among the birds, and the water was teeming with skipjack, yellow fin, and atule, large herring. All lines took hits almost immediately, and all three men fought to get their fish in. The excitement flowed like booze at a town beer club, and the men were drunk on it almost immediately. They pulled in their catches with a mixed chorus of shrieks, curses, mad laughs and giggles. The smell of the sea and engine exhaust, mixed with the aroma of fresh fish blood and sweat, to fill the men's lungs with the primeval scent of the hunt as the killing madness overtook them.

Getting the fish into the boat was only a part of the battle. The large yellow fin snapped, flipped, and jumped about the bilge; and pandemonium prevailed as each man fought to subdue his fish. The skipjack and atule were a bit smaller, quicker in their jumps and flips. Blood, fish and human, squirted, splashed and flowed over everything. The bilge turned red and filled with a foamy pink scum. Lines tangled and knotted as fish convulsed amid piles of nylon monofilament. To make matters worse, they had only one killing club, and had to take turns beating their catches senseless. The men prevailed, and the fish lay twitching in the bilges, smaller and more fragile than they had appeared just minutes before. The sea was empty, and the deep blue swells revealed nothing. They sat exhilarated, exhausted, nursing their wounds, and untangling the mass of line lying about the bilge. It took them a good half hour to make sense of the mess. All the time, Setu had been circling slowly, looking for sign of a school.

"There!" yelled Setu, pointing toward the west. Then, they were off again on the chase before the lines were even back in the water. It went on like this throughout the morning. They quickly learned how to get the fish aboard and quiet with less fuss. It allowed them to stay with the schools longer and catch more fish. They barely had time to think, let alone rest, between contacts with the schools. By anyone's standards, it was an extraordinary day of fishing.

<$<>$>

Around about noon the motor sputtered, started again, ran for a few minutes, sputtered again, and then chugged to a stop. They sat looking at one another blankly, coming out of the killing trance; the endorphin rush of the hunt silently evaporating in the cool chill of lonely ocean breezes. They looked quietly back and forth, eyeing one another, saying nothing, feeling the sudden heat of the bright sun, and catching heavy whiffs of fish blood and guts as the boat rolled and pitched over the deep inky blue prairie. There were only the sounds of the water lapping against the sides of the boat and the haphazard rolling of a coconut shell bailer in the bilges.

"What's wrong Setu?" asked Filo.

"I don't know. It stopped," said Setu, a bit bewildered.

"Give the cord a pull." suggested Sale.

Setu bent down and went through the ritual he had watched others perform. He squeezed the gas line bulb, pulled out the choke, and yanked the cord. To everyone's relief the engine caught immediately.

"Well, we got enough fish. What say we head back?" said Filo, trying not to sound panicky.

"Yeah, good thing to do," agreed Sale.

Setu swung the boat eastward toward the blue gray outline of the island, which suddenly appeared a distant and long journey over a sea of large dark swells.

"Setu, how far are we?" asked Sale a few minutes later.

"Far."

"How long?"

"Long."

The relief Sale had felt when the motor caught was dampened by Setu's terse replies. He looked off toward the purple mountains and wondered how they had managed to get so far out, so far from land, so far from home. Twenty minutes later, the motor sputtered to a stop again. Setu went through the ritual of pumping the bulb, pulling the choke, and pulling the cord. The engine chugged, sputtered, and died. He pulled the cord again and it caught. They moved off again toward the island, which shimmered in the distance at the top of each swell, appearing no closer than when they had first decided to head home.

Not ten minutes later, the engine died again. Setu went through his ritual to no effect. He pulled the starter cord again, and there was only the 'burrahh, barahh, puffahh! Puffahh!' sound of the cylinders cycling. Looking around at the other two men he pulled the cord again and then again. Each time it would fire once or twice and stop. Setu was not a man to panic; neither was he one change from an accepted course of action. He crouched at the engine, pulling on the cord, time after time, until his strong arms screamed for a break. Then he sat down in the bobbing boat and looked at Sale. "It's dead," pronounced Setu.

"Let it sit for a few minutes and then try again," said Sale quietly.

"The island is a long way off, isn't it?" said Filo, looking at the mountains anchored far beyond the most distant swells.

"Days of rowing," said Setu, matter-of-factly. "Wind and currents against us," he added, shaking his head. "Too far."

"Is that so!" said Filo in a cracking voice. "Pull the cord again!" he commanded in a near panic.

Setu stood and faced the engine. He performed the rituals again. It was to no effect. He pulled on the starter cord, once, twice, again and again; each pull, faster and with greater force than the one before. The flywheel turned, kept spinning by the pulls of the cord. The plugs would not fire and all the men heard was the dull, hollow 'PHEFFT! PheffT, phefft' of the pistons, cycling and recycling in their chambers. After ten minutes, the cord broke, and came flying out, hanging slack in Setu's hand. He stood there silent and sad eyed, still griping the black rubber handle, the frayed nylon cord hanging limply.

Setu sat down defeated. Filo let out a low moan. Sale watched the distant mountains to the east rise and fall as the boat floated with the long swell. He fought down a growing sickness.

"Let's eat," said Sale. "Then we'll think about what to do." He got one of the green coconut frond baskets from the bow and took out a baked taro and a cold greasy sausage. He passed the basket back to the others. Filo just shook his head and passed the basket to Setu. Setu took a large taro and a piece of baked fish and began to eat.

"Filo eat," said Sale. "We are going to have to row if we don't get the engine started. Eat! You are going to need it."

"I'm not hungry," whined Filo.

"Neither am I," replied Sale, feeling his stomach tighten with each roll and pitch of the boat. "Eat," he commanded.

Filo took some food and ate slowly.

"What do you think Setu?" asked Sale after a few minutes.

"When the cord breaks on Iosefo's, we can take the top off and then wrap the cord around the flywheel. He has a Johnson. This is Mercury. I don't know."

"Then we take the top off and find out," commanded Filo with great firmness.

It took them a half hour to get the cowling off the engine, because they had never done it. They had watched a man at Fisheries take it off and listened to him talk about the engine. It had all been so new to them. They had not understood what he was doing or watched closely. It

63

seemed impolite to confess their ignorance. Now they broke the latch holding the cover in place because they could not figure out how it worked. When they got the cover off, they were shocked to see a cage of shiny black metal surrounding the flywheel on the top of the engine.

It was then they discovered they had no tools for the motor. Engine tools had been supplied, but they were sitting in the shed, where the motor was to be stored. The only tools of any sort they could find in rummaging the gear were a sledgehammer and a fish knife. With no screwdriver or wrench, they realized they could do little. They tried wrapping the cord around the wheel and passing it back behind the posts of the 'cage', the handle would not fit through. Then they took the handle off the cord, only to find they still could not get the cord through its proper opening because of the knot at the end of the frayed cord. After cutting off the knot, getting the cord around all the posts, and through the proper openings, the one pull it allowed produced the same empty result. It was a tedious procedure to repeat.

"Maybe we should just knock the damn cage off!" said Filo in a panicky voice. He was willing to do anything to get home. It was fine to go fishing, and catch fish. He dreaded spending a night in the tossing boat.

"The cord's too short," said Setu. "I can't pull it enough to get it to turn over much. We need to use another cord, a longer one. I don't know. It might work. I'm not sure, Sale." he added sadly.

"Let's think about it." said Sale. He was in no hurry to break his new engine. It was only three days old, and he had a bundle of bank papers in his pusa lava-lava, wardrobe chest, at home. "Let's row for a while and think about this." he said almost to himself.

"Row!" screamed Filo, "We don't have to row if we can get the damn engine started. That damn black box!" he added, putting a mark of condemnation on the motor.

Sale looked sharply at his cousin, saying nothing. "Setu, get the oars." Setu got the oars from their place under the seats. Then he sat there looking around, not finding what he wanted. "Sale, do you know where the oarlocks are?" he asked.

"Oarlocks?" said Sale not comprehending.

"The place for the oars, Sale. The pins."

"Yes. Yes, I know Setu," said Sale. "I know. I don't know where they are. Let's look down here," he said pointing below the gunnels. They found long heavy dowels attached to little chains resting behind the side slats. Sale silently thanked the fisheries carpenter who had put them there so securely. The oars went in between the dowels. Setu rowed. He was awkward at first, and had better result as he learned the best angles. It was obvious the oars were too short for best effect. The boat did make some headway, and it was better than sitting there and drifting. Setu rowed for thirty minutes, and then Sale for another thirty. When it was Filo's turn, he whined about being sick.

"Why don't we beat that damn top off and get at the flywheel?" he said. "We don't have to row, if we get the engine running!"

"I don't know if it will help," said Sale.

"Better than rowing!" screamed Filo.

"What do you think, Setu?" asked Sale.

"I don't know. The cord is too short. If I could get a longer cord on, it might help. When the cord breaks, sometimes the engine will start if you can pull with a longer one."

"Then let's do it and stop wasting time rowing!" Said Filo in a pinched voice.

"Setu, perhaps we have something for the bolts? Let's look for something to help get them off," said Sale. The two men looked around the boat, trying to find something to help loosen the bolts. The only 'tools' they had were a sledge hammer and a knife.

"You are wasting your time. Just knock it off. Let's get it done and get going. Why worry about bolts, when it is the engine that won't start? Just knock off what is in the way. Let's get started and get home!" commanded Filo, once again.

Sale had developed a headache, and it would not go away. The sun and the bobbing around were making him sick. The rowing helped a little. It did not block out Filo's demanding whining, or the growing fear in his gut. He found he could not think straight. After listening to Filo bitch and complain for thirty minutes, he told Setu to go ahead and knock the protector cover off with the sledge. It took Setu ten minutes of beating on the engine to get the 'cage' off. It lay in pieces; ragged black hunks of metal glistening in the bloody bilge. It made Sale sick to look at them, and he leaned over the gunnels and retched.

"Oh fine! Now, you're sick!" said Filo. "Now, I'll get sick too," he complained.

Sale just stared sternly at him after he emptied his stomach, it was enough to silence Filo. Setu tried the longer rope, and the engine caught a few times. After a brief moment of hope, it died. Setu tried again, and again, but it wore him out, and even he realized pulling on the cord did no good. He sat back down, his head bowed, staring into the bilges, the disgrace of failure heavy on his soul.

"What else?" Sale asked Setu.

Setu took a deep breath and let it out despondently. "Plugs. I have seen the plugs foul. Maybe the plugs need cleaning. Could be plugs." He said nodding a bit as he looked at Sale and then shook his head. "I don't know, Sale," confessed Setu, his weather reddened eyes sad with defeat. "I just don't know anything."

"Where are the plugs?" asked Sale hesitantly.

"Over here, behind this stuff," said Setu pointing to a dual set of 'tables' sitting over a couple of plug wells. "Can't get at it with this stuff in the way."

"Well bust it up!" demanded Filo. "Damn Mercury isn't no damn good. All they are is boat anchors! It's those plugs, for sure. I have heard others in town complain about those Mercury plugs. Just bust off those 'tables', and let's get at those plugs!"

Sale sat silent, staring at his cousin, thinking of busting up more than his engine. He was reluctant to continue beating on the motor. He knew it did not make sense to destroy something he had just bought. He thought of the care he gave his truck. He had been tentative about it at first, learning from others in the village who owned trucks. The outboard should not be much different, and beating it with a sledgehammer, defied everything Sale had learned about engines. But the sickening pitch of the swells, the raw heat of the sun, the occasional chill wind, and the distant blue outline of the island, made such thoughtful common sense disappear in a shudder of fear and dread at being adrift forever.

In the end, Setu did just as Filo had demanded. Sale had no better suggestion and just wanted his cousin to shut up. So, they busted the plug protectors and threw more metal into the bottom of the boat. Then, Sale sat there feeling stupid, when he realized they had no plug wrench with them. They had once again acted with no real purpose in mind. Filo laughed and made a remark about bad packing of the boat. Then he whined when Sale told him to row. Sale touched his cousin lightly on the shoulder and looked him deep in the eyes. One look at Sale's face convinced Filo rowing would be wise.

<><>

They took turns and rowed toward the island for over two days. The outline of the mountain ridges grew ever so slowly. The fish, their amazing catch, rotted quickly, forcing them to throw it overboard. It was a sad and messy job. However, it lightened the boat, and the stink had become overpowering. The rotten fish were reluctant to leave the boat, and floated after them like lost puppies, attracting predators, and for a while, they rowed the boat surrounded by long dark shapes cutting the water, and charging the boat ominously. Even these tired of the slow progress of the small boat, and drifted off.

The days were blisteringly hot. The light shirts and frond visors they had on did little to hide them from the sun and the wind, and the men slowly cracked and split open like overdone roasted pigs. The chilly nights brought fits of shivering, and allowed little sleep. They ran out of food and water on the evening of the second day. Finishing the last of the water turned their ill fortune into a matter of survival. Setu and Sale became silent as their situation became grimmer. Filo chattered on, complaining about everything, continually denouncing the engine—sitting forlornly on the rear transom, a sad ghost of its former self—while refusing to do his share of the rowing. Blisters he said. All three cousins had blisters.

During one rant, Filo criticized Sale for fishing so far out, and then he started making fun of Setu for not knowing anything about outboards and not much of anything else. It was the breaking point. Sale jumped up, grabbed his cousin by the throat and threatened to rearrange his head, and toss him overboard. Setu was right behind him, waving the killing stick in the air, laughing madly and letting Filo know how long he would float before a shark got him. The little scene did wonders to improve Filo's attitude and limit his chatter. Yet, even his quiet was an aggravation to the others as he made it clear he felt persecuted by his cousins.

On the last night, they could see the island distinctly by the light of the stars; a huge blackness, with a band of light along the horizon. Despite the difficult journey, they survived, and they managed to reach the little bay of the village before dusk in just over the three days Setu had predicted. They were a burned, thirsty, and beaten crew. They were home, and it was a small miracle no one could deny. As they approached the shore, a crowd gathered as word of their return spread across the village. Sisifo and the children rushed to the shore in tears. Sale was close to crying. Setu's wife and children were on the shore. They held back, avoiding the crowd, and waiting as Setu started unloading the gear before the boat had even hit the sand. The three-day delay did not change the need to unload the boat. It was work, and he knew work.

Filo perked right up when he found he had an audience. He talked loudly and told a tale. He condemned the Mercury outboard and claimed it was only good as a boat anchor. All in the crowd shook their heads in sympathy as he told how 'that damn black box' betrayed them when they needed it most. He pointed out the large chunks of metal they beat from the engine in retribution for its traitorous failure. His speech would have carried the day, had it not been for Setu's ten-year-old son, Iosefo.

Half listening to Filo's oratory, and helping his father carry gear from the boat, he suddenly started laughing wildly. "Hey Setu" he said loudly. "I know why the engine quit. I can tell you why." There, loud enough for half the village to hear, he blurted out between giggles. "No gas! You ran out of gas. This can is empty!" he shrieked holding the large red gas can high above his head to show its lightness.

As thanks, Setu reached across the boat, and cuffed him across the head so firmly it sent him sprawling into the shallow water. It was something he would much regret later, though had little control over. If it had not been for Tina, Setu's wife, he would have given Filo a severe beating, right there, in front of the entire village.

For Sale, it was the final stroke, the confirmation the nightmare was everything he had dreaded it would be. He was too tired to feel humiliated, thankful for Sisifo's soft hand as she led him away from the crowd, to feel anything but relief at being home, being with his family and being out of that damn boat.

70

Archimedes Fish Fry

Ulavale Pisupo sat in a small fale at the back of his wife's family compound, eating a meager meal of boiled green banana covered in salty coconut cream sauce, a few small reef fish he had speared that morning, and a strong cup of tea from a large white enameled metal cup decorated with bright purple and red tulips painted around the outside. His mind was not fully on the food, which was good, because the banana were still a bit raw, the pe'epe'e, coconut sauce, was a bit too salty, the small fried reef fish, mushy, and the tea tasted of soap. Ulavale was thinking of more complex matters than food. He was trying to figure out how to scrape together a few tala to take his daughter to the hospital in town, and money was not something to which he had easy access.

His options were few and equally unpleasant. He could go to Moipune, the matai, chief, of his family, his wife's eldest brother and ask for it. Moipune was an arrogant man, who preferred to spend money on himself, and who would make a great scene when Ulavale asked for a few tala, and likely not give it to him, despite his need. Worse, he would order Ulavale to work in his high plantation for another week, just out of spite.

Another possibility would be to go to the Priest and explain his problem. The Father was a good man and generous, though penniless as a result. In all likelihood, Father George would offer him a cup of coffee and pray with him. He liked the Father, for he was a gentle man. He would not likely have cash, and it was foolish to ask where there was no chance of receiving. Then, there was Pulemanu, a chief in the village, who owned a fishing boat. Ulavale could go out fishing with Pulemanu and be paid in fish, or perhaps some tala. Pulemanu was a difficult man. He knew he was one of the few places Ulavale could turn for cash, and he made Ulavale pay dearly. It would be long, demanding, and strenuous work, and in the end, he would barely get what he needed.

Ulavale sat cross-legged on the mats, eating his small meal off a section of a green banana leaf, thinking about his unpleasant choices. The child was sick, and the illness had not gotten better in the last week as he had hoped. She was now unable to eat her food, and what she did eat, came flying out the other end. His wife, Pesemalie, did what she could, it was obvious there was little they could do here in the village. A trip to the district hospital had not helped either. The district doctor had only told him what he already knew. He needed to take the child to the hospital in town. The money must be made. He was tired of working long hours in the hills for his brother-in-law and begging him would likely be useless anyway. There was only one option open to him. There had never been a choice. Ulavale felt better for considering what few choices he had; it gave him reason to do what no rational man would likely choose to do otherwise.

He thanked his wife for the meal, grabbed his walking stick and limped toward the house of Pulemanu. Ulavale walked about a hundred yards and rested a bit. His right leg was weak, and on occasion, like now, he found he needed to rest it while the tingling subsided. When it was better, he moved on. The sun was high in the sky and cast a blinding glare off the white sand of the village paths. He pulled his coconut frond hat down over his eyes and marched on.

Pulemanu's fale was large and of 'European' style, meaning it was a square mostly open sided concrete building with a corrugated metal roof. When he got there, Ulavale crouched outside the fale, muttered an abject greeting and waited. He could see Pulemanu inside and knew the man was aware of his presence. Pulemanu was a big man in the village, so Ulavale had to wait. He crouched in the sun for a few minutes, and a young boy came to the door. The boy knew Ulavale. He smiled and asked him how he was.

"I am fine, thank you Simione," replied Ulavale. "And how are you?"

"Good, thank you. The dog had puppies, and I will keep one as my pet," replied the boy.

"Good. Let it stay with its mother for some time, else it will sicken and die."

"I will remember Ulavale, thank you. You come to see Pulemanu?"

"Yes, I am here to speak with the chief." Before the boy could reply, a harsh yell from inside the fale chased him from the doorway. "The game begins," thought Ulavale sadly.

Pulemanu knew why Ulavale was at his door, and he was quite glad for it. The man was a good worker and fisherman, his occasional fits notwithstanding. Pulemanu could always use Ulavale in his boat. But, Pulemanu was a big man in the village, and it did no good to show he needed anyone, particularly one as lowly as Ulavale. So, he acted like he was scarcely aware the man huddled in the sun at the bottom of the steps. After making him wait outside for some time, he acknowledged Ulavale.

"Oh! Solē you come?" said Pulemanu using the term for untitled men.

Ulavale heard the call and slowly got down, crab-climbing the steps to the front door of the fale. He took the last few on his knees. resting his forearms on the floor of the fale and hanging his head low. "Yes, I come. Greetings to you great chief Pulemanu. Great respect I pay to such a chief as you," he replied.

"Yes. Yes. I am a very busy man. There are many things I must do," said Pulemanu confirming his own importance. "Get to the point, Solē. What is it you are wanting of me. I have little time for such as you."

"Honorable Pulemanu, I am seeking the opportunity of joining you on your fishing boat when you next go out."

"Solē, many men want to go fishing in my boat," lied Pulemanu. "Why should I take such as you?"

"Pulemanu, I have worked for you many times. You know I will work well. I catch many fish," said Ulavale stating the truth.

"Many people catch fish and work well, you are no exception," replied Pulemanu, once again telling a lie.

74

"I will come early, to load the boat and work late, cleaning it for you, sir."

"Ohhh! Solē. You say these things, yet you do not always choose to work for me. Why is that, Solē? Why do you come to me now, when all last week you did not come at all?"

"Pulemanu, your honor, I had family obligations. I spent many days in the high hills working on our family plantations. Only that has kept me from taking advantage of the grand opportunity you offer by giving me a place in your boat," said Ulavale, only half lying in return.

"You work all week in the plantations, and you do not even bother to bring me a basket of taro? I, who am so helpful to you, so often? You sadden me, Solē, that you would so quickly forget my beneficence." said the chief, wishing he had some taro to eat with his evening meal. "And now you expect me to once again show you great kindness by allowing you to fish in my boat?"

The statement was so outrageous Ulavale could not find an answer. He simple crouched silent, on the steps.

Finding he could wheedle no taro from the man, Pulemanu returned to the standard script. "What is it you want of me? A place in the boat, for some part of the catch? So be it," he said offhandedly, quietly satisfied he could give Ulavale almost nothing for his work and pocket the profit. It would make up for the taro the man failed to bring him, he thought peevishly.

"Honored chief, please, there is something I must also ask of you," said Ulavale in a low muttered voice Pulemanu understood only because of the comment's place in the degrading play they acted out.

"Get on with it, man, can you not see I am busy," replied the chief

"Sir, I am needing some tala, for this service you are allowing me to perform. I am thankful for your most generous offer of a part of the catch. I am needing a few tala for the taking of my family to town. My daughter is sick, and I need to visit the hospital."

"Tala? It is not enough I offer you a place in my boat and some part of the catch, now you are asking for tala as well?" replied Pulemanu. If it had been any other of the untitled men who worked for him, he would have taken the tala from the thick wad of bills he always carried in his lava-lava, crumpled them up, and tossed them negligently on the floor before the groveling man. But, this was Ulavale, one who had fits, fell on ground drooling and making noises. A man who would occasionally keel over and urinate on himself. Even his name, Ulavale Pisupo, Crazyhead Corned Beef, told the story of a time he had fallen down while carrying a large tin of pisupo into a great fiafia, a party of epic size. He had lay there, shaking and drooling, the can of pisupo still in his arms and resting on his chest. It was quite funny. Many in the village had gathered around to laugh and ridicule. It had become a village joke, and he was given the name Ulavale Pisupo as a remembrance of the event. No, it would not do to just throw money at such a one. "You must work for me twice if you want that many tala, Solē," he said smiling as he watched Ulavale's bowed head twitch at the news.

"As you say, honored chief. I will gladly go out in your boat twice. Tonight and once again when I come back from town. And for this you will give me three tala for the bus fares I need to go to town?"

76

"I wish you to work for me tonight and tomorrow as well. The price of fish is best before the weekend. You must work for me tomorrow, your trip to town can wait," ordered Pulemanu, taking pleasure in taunting the man.

"Great chief, my daughter is seriously ill. I must take my wife and child to the hospital as soon as possible. Please, to have some understanding of this," begged Ulavale.

"Solē! Always you have excuses! Yes, yes!" said Pulemanu, satisfied the man had groveled humiliatingly before him and now tiring of the game, wanting a nice nap. "Come to my house at 4:00, and you can load the boat. Now I am busy. Off with you!" said Pulemanu turning his back on front door.

"Thank you so much, honored chief, your kindness is greatly appreciated," muttered Ulavale as he touched his forehead to the floor of the fale and walked his knees back down the stairs until he could stand and not have his head above fale floor. He picked up his stick and made his way back home. The glare of the sun off the sand attacked his eyes as he walked, and he started to see arcs of geometric patterns spanning his vision. When he looked directly at something, it disappeared in a fuzzy collection of jagged gray geometric forms. He hurried, hoping the attack would not peak before he could make it back to the fale. He was in sight of his home when his right leg went tingly, and his right arm went numb. He pushed on, using his stick as a brace, the sounds of the day coming to him like he walked in a dream, and strange yet familiar thoughts and memories floated through his consciousness. He knew he had only a few minutes before he must either lie or fall down. A long difficult stretch of concentration, and he was at the fale. He ignored a call, grabbed a pillow and quickly lay on the mats as the seizure swept over him. Perhaps ten minutes later, he felt the disoriented unreality of the experience begin to ebb.

Pesemalie had seen him walking back to the fale. When she called to him and he did not answer, she understood what was happening. She had a cool cup of water waiting for Ulavale when he awoke. It was all she knew to do. When Ulavale sat up to drink his water, she was relieved to see he had not wet himself, as it always left him so sad.

"Iopa, It was a quick one," she said to him, using his Christian name as she watched him drink from the cup.

"I got home before it was bad," he said in response and took a long drink of water. "I go out with Pulemanu on his boat tonight. I will need a meal to take along."

"We have no tinned fish. I will ask Manulele for a can from the store."

"No need. I will eat before I go. There is taro, no?"

"Only the banana. Moipune has taken all the taro into his house."

"I will eat a hardy meal of green banana, then," he laughed. He will give me three tala for the work, added Ulavale, avoiding the fact he would have to fish twice. "We will take Alofa'ia to town tomorrow, to the hospital. She does not get better. Perhaps a European doctor can help. We will stay at my cousin's house."

"I have tried," said Pesemalie sadly.

"I know," said Ulavale, soothingly. "You are a good mother. Even so, the child sickens, and you are not well either. Now we must go to town. It will be all right," he said reaching out and touching her hand lightly. "Now, I will sleep for a few hours. It will be a long night in that old barge of Pulemanu's," he said with a smile and a sad shake of his head. He lay back down to sleep, feeling the secondary effects of the seizure coming back down on him.

<<>>

"Dear, it is time," whispered Pesemalie.

"Already? I go so far away for so short a time," he said as he smiled up at her. The seizure's hangover was almost washed from him by the deep sleep. He sat up and tasted the hot cup of tea his wife had placed before him. She brought him a meal of green banana, a small fried fish, a piece of breadfruit, and a few fatty pieces of fried meat, laid out on a fresh green banana leaf.

"The meat is from Manulele. She says thank you for helping unload the truck yesterday. Ulavale nodded and ate slowly; trying to get everything he could from the meal, knowing it would be a long night. Pesemalie had fixed him a meal for the night and put it in a woven green coconut frond bag. He put on his heavier fishing clothes—a thick lava-lava and an old flannel long sleeve shirt. He put the food and an old worn rugby jersey into a larger bag, said good-bye to Pesemalie, picked up his staff and slowly made the walk to Pulemanu's house.

When he got there he didn't bother to stop at the front fale. He went immediately to the back of Pulemanu's family compound, where there was a small shed with a padlocked door. He took the key from its place above the door and opened the storeroom. Inside was an assortment of fishing gear, an old engine, assorted cans and jugs, and a fifty-five gallon drum of gas.

He checked the gas in the main gas can and found it near full. He checked the water jug and found it needed filling. He grabbed the water jug and another just like it and limped slowly to the spring to fill them. After filling the water containers, he started carting gear down to the boat, which lay in the shallows just off the low mud-sand beach. It took him over an hour to cart the assorted equipment and supplies to the boat. It was back breaking and monotonous work, and though there were people about, no one offered to help, or even took much notice of him.

When he had the gear in the boat, he stowed and trimmed the load. He tightened down the old Archimedes outboard and connected the gas. It was a miserably slow engine. It ran regardless of the beating it took. He packed away the water and other gear and checked the rigs on each of the hand lines. When he finished, he walked back to Pulemanu's house and went to the entryway at rear. The boy met him at the steps, a small puppy in his arms.

"Talofa, Simione, that is a fine little dog," said Ulavale as he smiled at the boy and petted the tiny puppy.

"I have just taken it from its mother to show you, I will put him back in minute."

"That is good, see he has a tit to suck at, so he can get strong. Please tell Pulemanu the boat is ready."

"They are eating. I heard them talking. They know you have taken everything to the boat. I will tell Pulemanu it is ready."

"Thank you Simione." Ulavale could see Pulemanu, his son Paluvae, and Pulemanu's brother Samasoni, sitting in the fale eating while family members hurried about them, serving food. "I will wait in the boat," he said to the boy. He walked back to the shore, made a small bed out of a tarp, and lay down in the bow of the boat to rest until Pulemanu and the others arrived.

<<>>

"Ulavale, I do not pay you to sleep when you work for me! I should dock you fifty sene for the time you have slept here, rather than getting the boat ready," complained Pulemanu as he, Paluvae, and Samasoni waded out to the boat. "Look at this! The gear is not even in the right places," he lied. "And did you bring the food bags down from the fale? No! Why did you not bring the food from the fale? Go now and get the food baskets from the back of the fale. And hurry! We do not have all-night!"

"Yes sir," muttered Ulavale through the fog of his unrest. He slipped out of the boat and made his way back toward the fale.

"Here Ulavale!" said the boy. "They left the baskets here."

"Thank you Simione, may God bless you this evening."

"And may he bless you also, Ulavale, and may you have a safe trip," called the boy as Ulavale limped slowly back toward the shore.

"You have delayed us Solē! Your laziness is a great burden on me. Hurry! Get in the boat so we may leave!" complained Pulemanu. "No! No, you dimwit! First, untie the mooring line! Have you learned nothing about launching this boat?"

Ulavale, caught half in the boat, dropped back into the water, accompanied by the laughs of Pulemanu, his son, and brother, and waded to the front of the boat. He walked the line to the mooring rock, untied the rope and made his way back toward the boat. This was not something he wanted to do. He had left the oars out in the boat, so they might pole out. Now, trapped into getting wet, he dreaded the plague of night dampness and chills.

"No, no," said Pulemanu in disgust. "Guide us out of the shallows first you Ulavale! The engine needs more water under it. Solē, do you know nothing?"

Ulavale said nothing, not wishing to incite Pulemanu into further bluster. Instead he waded out into the bay until the water was at his chest, then came back to the boat, and hauled in unaided. He sat there dripping wet for a moment, before taking off his lava-lava and wringing it out into the bilges.

Pulemanu was busy starting the engine. Running it was a procedure he guarded against others. Only he knew enough about it to get it going and keep it running. After some puttering with the fuel line and a few pulls of the cord, the engine sputtered to a start and chugged roughly. The chief dropped it into gear and the boat pushed ahead slowly. It was an old engine, a Swedish made Archimedes two-stroke of less than five horsepower. It had run for many years and endured mistreatment that would have killed most engines. One of the simplicities of the engine was its air-cooling, the heat dissipated from the engine through a set of large aluminum cooling fins surrounding the single cylinder. These were so pronounced they gave the engine wings; the flat multiple plates sticking out on both sides of the engine looking like the stacked wings of the Red Barron's tri-plane.

Pulemanu bought the engine and boat from another chief in the village when the man became too old to go out fishing. He did little to maintain either. Both were built to take mistreatment, and though coming to the ends of their lives, they were still serviceable. The boat was old, built by a long dead craftsman. It was of a popular modified whaleboat design with a wide beam and a shallow draught, yet the capacity to cut through the seas well. A small high flat stern cut the risk of broaching in heavy following seas. A sound boat, built in a time when such was the main form of island transport. Now, it leaked and needed a refit; cried for recaulking, stripping, and repainting. It begged to have some of its support ribbing replaced. Pulemanu had no intent of doing any of this. However he was no fool. He took the old boat out only on calm evenings, and was quick to head back in at the slightest suspicion of bad weather. Despite these limitations the boat served its purpose well as a fishing platform.

The boat was power; it provided fish to the village, which gave him much influence and allowed him to sell some as well. It made Pulemanu one of the few people in the village with ready access to cash. It gave him the means to pay off the village higher chiefs, the pastor, and to indenture such men as Ulavale. A great source of power needed guarding. As much as Pulemanu hated fishing, he never let anyone else run the engine or take the helm from him. Lazy and conniving he might be; stupid he was not.

The boat slowly made its way across the lagoon and toward the cut in the reef. The swell came up a bit as it met the outer reef, and the cut was awash in white-water when they bounced high through the channel. Once outside there was not a ripple on the water as the sun cast its last rays across a mercury tinted sea. They were headed out a few miles, not far, but too far for those who fished these water in outriggers to venture. They frequented a large area of depth called the pu'ia, the fish hole, and had a couple of places along the edges they visited regularly.

"Bail Solē! Are you so lazy you cannot see the bottom is awash in water?" called Pulemanu, above the loud parf-parf-parf sound of the single cylinder Archimedes engine.

Ulavale bent down and picked up a bailer, a scoop fashioned from a plastic vegetable oil container, and started to bail the water from the boat. The others just sat inert, not speaking or doing anything of value. Neither Paluvae nor Samasoni enjoyed fishing. Pulemanu commanded they go and they obeyed. Neither was much of a fisherman. They did what was required and did so with mild resentment as they felt the entire venture below them, even though much of their status emanated from the fish Pulemanu brought back in the boat. They would handle a line, catch fish, and rest on the way back. That was all. The solē was there to do the rest. When Ulavale, or some other poor villager, was not along, Paluvai and Samasoni fought constantly over their responsibilities, each vying to do the least amount of work.

An hour of slow motoring across a calm sea brought them to a point where a triangulation off three islands that told them it was the edge of the Pu'ia. It was always an trial to find the right spot. They were close. They dropped the anchor over, set the lines, and started to fish.

Ulavale was first to haul in a fish. It was a small red snapper, its orange air bladder large in its throat like a thick distended tongue. Ulavale glanced at Pulemanu when he pulled it into the boat. The chief just stared at him, so he dropped it into the bilge. A few minutes later, he hauled in another one, just a bit smaller than the first. He said nothing, and the others made no comment. Camaraderie was not a characteristic of Pulemanu's boat.

After about an hour, fishing picked up slightly. Pulemanu made noises of discontent. Over an hour passed and they had caught only five fish. Pulemanu decided to move. Ulavale pulled up the anchor line. They got underway, heading toward what Pulemanu felt was the center of the lip of the pu'ia. They had run for perhaps five minutes, when the chief called to him.

"Solē, hand me those two small ones," said Pulemanu.

Ulavale looked around the bottom of the boat and saw the two small red snapper. He picked them up and handed them back to Pulemanu.

"You eat those Mu ?" he asked.

"You just do as I say. What I eat is not your concern," snapped Pulemanu.

Ulavale would have argued eating the fish under most circumstances because they were known to be poisonous from time to time. It was never certain when the fish would be bad to eat, and many fishermen did not eat Mu at all, or at least without first feeding it to a dog or cat, to see if it was poisonous; others just watched the moon or the seasons, and avoided the fish during 'dangerous' times. The Mu might not always be poisonous, but under the right circumstances, it could be deadly.

Pulemanu knew the stories of the Mu. He had gotten a bit sick a time or two from eating them. It was never anything too serious, and he had never seen anyone get too sick. He had never seen a cat or dog die of eating one either. He gave little credence to what he had come to regard as mostly folklore, which only fetched him less money for some of the fish he caught. He hated selling some of the catch at lower prices. Anyway, he liked the taste of the small Mu; and for Pulemanu, taste was an important determinant of his diet.

Ulavale simply did as told and without protest, for he was fed-up with Pulemanu and his family. He expected to work and to do so for less than others might earn. Today he needed money, and Pulemanu was being bad to him, and his son and brother had helped not at all.

Pulemanu spit on the cooling fins of the motor, and they sputtered and sizzled. He laughed. As the others watched him he jammed the two small fish into the openings between the top cooling plates, one on each side of the motor. The fish stared back at the crew, mouths gaping large, eyes wide open. It seem they were screaming in agony and begging for release from the Archimedes torture-grill. They sizzled and smoked, and even as the boat motored into the wind, the sweet marine smell of grilling fish filled the boat. They ran for twenty minutes. Pulemanu shifted the engine into neutral and stood, gazing toward the dark shadows of the islands. "This is good," he said as he shut the motor off and motioned Ulavale to drop the anchor. "Now we can have a feed."

"Palu, hand me the plates," commanded Pulemanu. He took a knife from the ribbing below the gunnels and scraped the char-fried fish out of the space between the cooling fins of the engine and onto the plates. It smelled good. Pulemanu smiled and divided one fish, giving some each to Paluvae and Samasoni. The bigger of the two fish he kept on his plate. He did not even look at

Ulavale who only existed when something needed doing. "Sole," he said. "Pass me the jug of water and the food bags, and get the lines over." He took the water and a long swig, and passed it to Paluvae. Opening the food bag, he placed some breadfruit and a bit of palusami, (baked taro leaves and coconut cream), on the plates. He passed a plate to Palu and one to Samasoni. The three sat in the gentle swell, eating their meal and telling stories. There was no plate for Ulavale, who simply continued fishing.

"That was good," exclaimed Pulemanu after he had eaten the meal. "Palu, you liked that, yes? I thought so. Good, no Samasoni? Just what we needed to change our luck. Solē, you should have brought a plate. It was a good fish fry. Too bad you missed out," he said with joking sarcasm. He and the others laughed. It was a funny joke.

Ulavale said nothing as he pulled up his line, heavy with a fish. He had begun catching fish immediately. It appeared a good spot. The others finished their meals and threw their plates into the bilge for him to clean, then they dropped their lines overboard. Soon they too were catching fish, though less frequently than Ulavale. They fished for about an hour, sometimes busy and others in lull. During one of the lulls, Pulemanu farted loudly.

"Oh! What a sounding of the shit horn! I make great gas tonight," he giggled.

Paluvae hooked a fish and was pulling it in when suddenly he bent over the boat and puked into the water. He sat down on the bench, letting the line go. Ulavale was next to him and reached over and grabbed the line, then wrapped his own line around an oar to hold it, and pulled in Paluvae's line. Before he had it to the surface Paluvae was leaning over the side again, dry heaves wracking his body.

"What is wrong with you Paluvae? There is not even a swell tonight. You should not be puking in these seas," complained Pulemanu.

"I do not feel so good," was all Paluvae could moan between gags.

Pulemanu laughed and farted loudly. This time he made no joke about it. "Damn!" he said, "I have shit myself!" He moved to stand. Before he could get upright, he farted again. "Damn!" he said again as fluids ran down his legs. He started to unwrap his lava-lava and suddenly bent over as a cramp racked his gut. It forced him back down, and he sat unwillingly in his own mess. He passed gas and fluids. "Ooohhh!" he groaned, "I am sick. I am hurting very bad in my stomach."

Pulemanu's brother, Samasoni, who had said nothing all night, suddenly let out a loud belch. "Funny taste in my mouth, I am so thirsty," he said before belching again and suddenly projecting a large stream of vomit into the bilge.

"Over the side you idiot," commanded Pulemanu, through his own pain. "Now we must put up with your stink."

"You shit all over the boat," rasped his brother as he leaned over the gunnels and puked again. "You are stinking worse than a dead pig and you scold me for a little puke? To hell with you!"

"It is my...," said Pulemanu responding to his brother before a cramp doubled him over again, and he let out a large liquid fart. "It is my...," he tried again, spewing into the bilges, unable to get his head over the side. "Oh God!

What is happening?" he complained as he puked again, and farted loosely.

An evil smell filled the boat as all three men were overcome with dire sickness. All three vomited violently, emptying their guts, and then gaged and dry heaved in prolonged agony. Alternating shivering and sweats overcame them, and they soon collapsed into the filthy, fish strewn bilges, forced into fetal positions by a strange assortment of aches and pains.

Soon Paluvae was complaining of numbness in his hands and feet. Then, when he moved, he screamed of a terrible burning on his skin. The boy became almost hysterical, and on one occasion, he almost climbed out of the boat before Ulavale could calm him down. As the vomiting and diarrhea ebbed, chills, sweats, numbness, and strange sensations on the skin became complaints.

Ulavale was not effected by the illness hitting the others, and he simply kept on fishing, catching one fish after the next, throwing them into the bottom of the boat, alongside the sick men. Pulemanu realized they needed to get to shore. When he called Ulavale, he was greeted with a strange vision of half-man and half-fish. He was not afraid. He wondered why Ulavale should look so. He ordered Ulavale to pull in the lines and the anchor rope. Ulavale complied. Pulemanu watched him sit in the bow, the gills in his neck moving in and out as he breathed. He stared transfixed as Ulavale ate baitfish from a woven bag of seaweed.

Pulemanu tried to get up, finding his legs and arms too sore, and the joints hurting terribly. The boat drifted for some time before Pulemanu could even try to start the engine. When he did he found just trying to stand caused so much pain in his legs it bent him over. He was hallucinating and head the fish at the bottom of the boat talking badly about him. He could see some of them making faces at him. The pain in his arms and hips was so great he stumbled against the engine, and sat again in the bottom of the boat. The boat drifted for another long period before Pulemanu was able to ask Ulavale to help him get the motor started.

"I know nothing of this motor," said a fish faced Ulavale to Pulemanu. "I cannot start it."

"Ulavale you have eaten too many of those shiners, you are looking like one," said Pulemanu. "I will show you how to start this," moaned Pulemanu, through his pain and headache.

"And if I get it started, then you will steer it home?"

"You must drive it home, I am hurting too much," moaned Pulemanu from the bottom of the bilge.

"I know nothing of this. You wish me to start your engine, and to steer your boat home. And if I make a mistake, you will hold me responsible? I can see the island, it is better I row back," he said.

"No, no. To row will take too long. We are all too sick. Can you not see how sick we are? We need to get home quickly. I will reward you well for your help. Please get us home quickly."

"Pulemanu, this is not the first time you have promised to reward me well. Your intentions always change when we get home. You say things to me, and then you do not do as you say you will. What makes now any different? I am thinking when we get back, it is me you will blame for this mess in the boat, and it is I who you will expect to

90

clean it. And if anything happens to your boat, you will hold me responsible for the damages. You remember the rig you let slip over the side many months ago? Then, when we got back to the village, I paid the price. I fished for nothing that night, not even a fish for my family. You thought it was funny to send me home with nothing. You remember?"

"Oh! Ulavale I hurt too much for such talk! My body hurts. I do not wish to speak about these things, and my head aches badly, worse than any long night's drinking, I think. Please just help us. I will do whatever you want! I promise."

"Your promises are hollow, Pulemanu. You will give me the money I ask for tonight, will you not."

"Yes! The money I will give right now! Anything! Just get me home!" pleaded Pulemanu.

"And I will not work for another day on your boat. Someone else will clean this mess," added Ulavale disdainfully. "You will give me the money tonight, before we leave the boat," he demanded, knowing how Pulemanu liked to cheat him.

"Yes, yes, whatever you say," moaned Pulemanu.

"And an oso, a gift, for my family, for the trip to town. You will give me two ten tala notes as a gift of thanks, to wish me well on my trip. Yes!", demanded Ulavale remembering Pulemanu's pleasure in forcing him to work when he needed to take his daughter to the hospital.

"Yes, yes, just get us home! Please! Oh, Please! Ulavale, I beg you to help me! Anything, if you only get me back to the village and out of this boat!" wept Pulemanu.

"OK, Pulemanu, I will try. Remember, I am not as smart as you, and though I would prefer to row, I will drive this engine of yours and steer the boat."

With Pulemanu's occasional direction, Ulavale managed to get the engine started, and after some experimentation, he figured out how to steer the boat, managed to turn it toward the shore and head it on an uncertain path back toward the village. As time passed, the men got worse, with terrible headaches, burning skin, and fits of uncontrolled shivering and pain becoming frequent.

Almost two hours passed before the boat came in sight of the lights of the village. Ulavale's apprehension grew. Pulemanu had fallen silent and lay in the bilges at his feet. His son was almost as quiet, but still groaned occasionally, and Samasoni lay face up near the bow, breathing heavily. Getting through the cut in the reef was always difficult, and even Pulemanu had some narrow escapes with waves tossing them one-way or the other, getting them close to the coral heads. Ulavale, for all the times he had been aboard the boat and made the passage, became confused when it came time for him to pilot the craft through. The swell, which had appeared so mild when out beyond the reef, now formed into seemingly great walls of water braking and cascading in front of where Ulavale thought the channel should be.

After motoring in circles just outside the breakers, he realized he could time the entry to the cycle of the swell. He was so preoccupied with handling the boat, it was difficult for him to accurately count the waves in darkness of the night. On two occasions he started in, only to drop off a swell early, when he suddenly realized it was far too big to ride through the cut.

Ulavale decided he must take his chance, and after watching two sets go rolling in, he made his move. The boat caught a wave and started through the narrow reef channel. As the wave broke, the boat turned into the wave, yawed, and started to slide sideways down the wave. Confused, Ulavale pulled the rudder toward him rather than pushing it away, and the boat turned farther into the wave, threatening to capsize. He quickly adjusted, but the damage had been done, and though the boat remained upright, it slid along the wave, almost out of control, pushed far from the center of the channel. After some severe bumps and knocks as it bounced over coral heads, it came to rest in the shallows, far outside the channel.

Ulavale looked around the boat. Water sat six inches deep, gear and fish swirled around the bilge. The hull appeared whole, though the engine prop was broken. He dropped into the water and tried to guide the boat back into the channel. Even in the surge of larger sets, the water was not deep enough for him to work the boat out of the coral bound pool in which it had become stranded. Too tired to push or pull, he gave up.

"Pulemanu I must go for help. The boat is stuck," said Ulavale. Pulemanu did not reply or respond when shook. "Paluvae! Paluvae do you hear me?" he asked of the son. Paluvae only moaned. "I must go for help. I will take my payment now. Do you hear me?" Paluvae only moaned.

Reaching down, Ulavale undid the stinking lava-lava from around Pulemanu's large waist and untied the knot at its upper corner. In it Pulemanu had the roll of money he always carried. Ulavale counted out three tala for the evening's work and found two ten-tala bills buried deep in the wad. He took those too. "I have taken my pay and the oso promised to me. Paluvae, do you understand? Pulemanu and I agreed to this. "The boy moaned. Ulavale reached down and shook him roughly. "I have taken my payment. Nothing more! Do you hear me? "The boy whined in pain at the touch. "Do you hear me?" repeated Ulavale shaking him again, wanting no accusations of wrong doing to follow him off the boat.

Paluvai screamed as Ulavale shook him. "Don't touch me. Oh it burns so! Yes! Yes, I understand. Please, please Ulavale! Help me! Please," he cried.

"I go for help, now," said Ulavale as he wadded the money and tied it in a shirttail. Satisfied it would not come undone, he collected his gear. He would leave nothing of his in the boat. When he had his things gathered, he took one last look around the boat, finding he had little concern for the fortunes of the three men who lay in the bilges.

Ulavale dropped into the water and swam and waded his way over the reef shallows, and then across the narrow lagoon toward the shore. It took him almost an hour to get to the village. He went directly to the house of Pulemanu and woke the family. He told them what had happened, that the men were sick, and described the location of the wrecked boat.

He was cut and bleeding from his effort to free the boat and the walk through the shallows. No one took notice. No one cared. He left the family to sort out its problems in the early morning darkness and walked home feeling tired and weary.

<<>>

Pesemalie awoke surprised to see Ulavale come into the fale so early in the morning. She moved to get up. He told her to stay on the mats, and said he would join her soon. He put his money in a safe place, went to the pool, took a bath, and cleaned the cuts and scrapes. He returned to the fale and crawled under the mosquito net to join his wife and child. In a hushed voice he related what had happened, and asked her to prepare for the long trip to town in the morning. "We will leave on the late morning bus," he whispered to her as the weariness of the night crept up on him. Then he fell asleep.

<<>>

When he woke in the morning, the village was abuzz with the news of the night's calamity on Pulemanu's boat. He quickly learned from the chatter outside the fale, all three men had been taken to the district hospital. The boat had been dragged to its mooring. The reports were Pulemanu's son was the least sick. It was feared Pulemanu might not survive. Samasoni was in less severe condition than Pulemanu and was expected to recover. Ulavale received the news without emotion, and realized he did not care if Pulemanu lived or died.

Pesemalie told him everyone in the village knew he had brought the boat back. She told him she heard no bad words being spoken about him. Most thought he had gotten only less ill. The concern, however, was for

Pulemanu, for he was such an important man in the village.

Ulavale sat his wife down and spoke to her quietly. "You must take whatever is important to you. Pack the chest with just what you will need, leave the rest. We will stay in town and not come back."

Pesemalie, who had only been to town a few times, was surprised. "Why is this, Iopa? What causes you to want to leave the village?"

"I tire of working for Pulemanu and serving your brother, Moipune, who has not been honest with us. The child is sick. You do not do well either. No, no, Pese do not deny it," he said quieting her tenderly. "Few here care for us. We must leave this place, or our family will wither like leaves in the heat of the sun. Some say town is a demanding place. It can be no worse than what we have found here. My cousin will help as much as he can, and he has said he will make a place for us in his fale. I am told there is always work in town for a man who can labor honestly and steady. I have worked all my life. I am sure I can do so there. We will live better than we do here."

"As you say," said Pesemalie, who feared for her daughter and had learned to distrust her elder brother.

Ulavale, walked slowly to the spring pool to bath. The cuts on his legs were not deep. There were gashes on his feet, causing him to limp more than usual. The water was cool and settled his body and mind, despite the difficult decisions he had made. He let the water surround him, feeling its crisp freshness saturate him. When he finished he limped back toward the fale, resting on his staff occasionally.

96

"Ulavale! Ulavale Pisupo! Come and talk with me!" called his brother-in-law Moipune, from his large fale at the front of the family compound.

Ulavale stopped and gazed into the dark interior of the fale of the chief, not wanting to approach.

"Come! Come and talk with me. I wish to have words with you, Ulavale," called Moipune from the shadowed darkness of the fale.

Ulavale stood silent staring at the fale. Then, reaching a quiet decision, he limped to the rear of the house and stood there.

"Come, sit down," urged his brother-in-law.

Ulavale struggled up the steps and sat down, his back against the doorpost. It was as far into the fale as he cared to go, or was welcome, for that matter. The fale was empty; most of the woven coconut side blinds were down to block out the heat and light of the morning sun. Only Moipune sat there in the darkened interior.

"Ulavale, I hear you are a great hero today. You saved Pulemanu, his son, and his brother. That is good. For once, you bring honor to our family. You are a burden on me, you know. Now you do a good thing. I am proud for you. But, Ulavale," said Moipune sadly shaking his head. "I am also hearing you received three tala for working for Pulemanu last night. Is that right?"

"Yes," said Ulavale, his anger suddenly hot within him.

Moipune made a chicking sound with his cheek against his teeth, shaking his head again, expressing regret. "Ulavale, I am surprised at you. I am your chief. Should it not be your wish and pleasure to present that money to me? You know I guard your welfare, and I am the one who handles cash for this family," said Moipune graciously.

"The money is to take my daughter and Pesemalie to the hospital. They are sick and need care," responded Ulavale.

"That is as it may be. Ulavale, I am your chief, and it is for me to decide how that three tala will be spent. After all, you are not one who has been worthy of much respect. You fall down and pass water on yourself. It is a great disgrace to the family. It is important I see to your well-being. Do you understand?"

"Yes Moipune. I understand."

"Then, you will give me the money!" commanded Moipune.

"No," said Ulavale without apparent emotion.

"What?" replied Moipune shocked and suddenly angry about the theft of his money. "You deny me? You know the way things are Ulavale. You have nothing I, Moipune, your chief, have not seen fit for you to have, nor can I not take back from you. This is my household. I know what is best for you, for my sister, and the little one. It is for me to decide when you go to town, or to the hospital, and not something you should be deciding on your own. The money must be given to me in any case," he added quite satisfied with the justness of his speech.

"No," said Ulavale staring at the man, "No, Moipune, you will get nothing from me. Pesemalie, your sister, sickens. so does the child. You know this and have done nothing to help. I have labored well for this family, and you care not for us. There is nothing you have promised you have

98

not reneged on or lied about. I am finished with you Moipune."

"Ulavale," laughed Moipune ignoring his complaints. "You will make it very harsh on yourself! Do you not see this? I am your chief! There is no one else in the village you can turn to. I will make your life exceedingly difficult, you know."

Ulavale looked at the man, straightening his back, looking eye to eye with the chief. "I understand Moipune. I understand that you have already made my life difficult. I am done with you. I am done with this retched village as well. And, hear me Moipune, I understand much more than you may think. I understand that if you play games with me, you will play by my rules not yours. I understand, if you step in my way, or do anything to hurt Pesemalie, your wife will learn of the whore you sleep with in town. And Faitagi," continued Ulavale, referring to a powerful high chief of the next village, "will know of your regular pinching of his upland taro. And Saifune," he added, mentioning another chief in the village, "will know where his two cases of pisupo disappeared to last month. I understand these things and a great many more, Moipune. Now the question is do you understand, and do you want others to understand as well?"

"No one would believe such as you! I do not fear your understandings," lied Moipune.

"Then let us dance. We will see who is burned by the tossing of the knife," said Ulavale referring to the twirling dance of the fire knife.

Moipune said nothing else and sat in the darkened fale, shocked Ulavale would speak to him as he did, enraged that he could do nothing to stop the man from leaving the village; for there were many more things he sought to conceal and which he feared Ulavale could reveal.

"Fine," said Ulavale. "It is good so much understanding now comes between us, brother of my wife." Ulavale stared unblinking at Moipune until the chief looked away. He stared through the silence until the chief glanced back at him. Ulavale fixed him once again with a grim stare. He slowly pointed a finger at Moipune, whose eyes widened ever so slightly at such an insult. "Now, I prepare to leave this place, and you, Moipune, will not interfere."

Ulavale let his words echo through the empty fale and settle into the silence. Then, still staring at Moipune, he took up his walking stick and stood silently, his head rising above the sitting chief. Without even a nod, he turned his back on Moipune, limped down the steps, and hobbled slowly back to his small fale.

He packed a few hand tools, a couple of old mother-of-pearl fishing lures, an ancient octopus lure that had once been his great-grandfather's, some hooks, a bollard of line, some heavily mended clothing, and a white lava-lava and white shirt. That was all there was. These things were placed at the bottom of the wooden chest. He called little else his own. He put on a well-worn clean lava-lava, a mended shirt, and a pair of rubber slippers, old and brittle, the cracks sewed together with fishing line. Pesemalie packed her clothes, the baby's clothing, some bedding, a picture of her mother and father, two china cups and saucers that were gifts from her mother, and a few kitchen implements. She wore her village women's committee dress, the only good dress she owned, besides her white church clothes. That was all.

Ulavale asked Pesemalie's cousin to help him haul the chest to a tree by the road. Pesemalie sat on the chest in the shade of the tree, Alofa'ia fussing uneasy in her arms. Ulavale squatted on his haunches nearby, methodically smoking a rolled brown paper bag cigar made with local tobacco. The sweet harsh smoke burned itchy-hot as it went down his throat. He had come to appreciate its raw bite.

Pesemalie's cousin and his wife came out to see them off. They brought along a small food bag and a bottle of water, a gift for the long trip to town. No one else took any notice of their impending departure.

As they sat there under the tree a pickup truck came roaring down the road. It pulled up in front of the great fale of Pulemanu, and a brother-in-law of Pulemanu jumped out and hurried into the fale. Suddenly howls and cries of grief and despair rose from the fale.

Ulavale stared out over the lagoon toward the distant reef. He took a long drag on his cigar and let the biting smoke drift from his lungs. His only thought was that such grief was better than the poisoning a poor cat or dog.

The bus arrived in a pall of dust and exhaust smoke, while loud lamenting and cries still echoed from the house of Pulemanu. Ulavale, his wife's cousin, and the bus driver's helper, loaded the chest onto the roof of the old bus and tied it down. He paid the driver fifty sene each, for himself and Pesemalie and a tala for the chest. The isle was already crowded with bags of taro and baskets of banana, and they climbed slowly over them until they found their place near the back of the half-full bus.

The bus pulled out, its engine roaring, gears straining, a dark cloud of exhaust and sandy dust billowing about it. Ulavale, sitting on the wooden bench next to Pesemalie, took a long drag off the stub of his cigar. He stared intently out the bus window at the village. As the house of Pulemanu went by he reached behind Pesemalie and the child and flicked the large roach out the window. 'Good riddance Ulavale Pisupo!' he thought as he let out a deep lung full of bitter-sweet smoke, and then he prepared himself for the long rough ride to town.

By Hook and Line

S auaso looks out over the gun-metal predawn waters of the Pacific awakening from a rough night. The swell had thundered against the reef throughout the night, had settled to a growl, no longer sending long barrels of white-water rumbling along the outer reef. He stares out into the sky, toward the horizon, searching for unrest in the blackness and grayness of a false dawn. The heavy squalls of the night have marched to the west, followed by tamer cloud heads, milder threats of rain. He smells the air, letting the sea tell him its story, then turns and looks inland toward the high dark uplands of the island. Their outlines uncluttered by mountain clouds. All appears well, the omens positive, nothing vibrates with danger, or demands too much caution. It suddenly irks him they are still on the beach, will not be underway at first light. He flushes irritably along the backs of his arms and legs, the heat agitating his thoughts. He looks around, spying Salanoa, who is carrying an armful of gear, aims a sharp whisper at him, making it clear he holds the man accountable for the delay.

"Hurry! Hurry, I do not want to spend all morning on the beach! You keep dragging, and we won't be back before dark!" he chides Salanoa. Sauaso shakes his head and marches off down the beach to find a secluded spot. Salanoa, unfazed, does not change his pace, his expression or bother to reply. He knows Sauaso, always impatient, always hot to be on his way, always growls in the early morning. Salanoa knows the comments only reflect Sauaso's need to be gone from the village, to be fishing.

Salanoa drops gear in the boat, realizes the heavier equipment has yet to be loaded and heads back toward the storage shed behind Sauaso's main family fale. "Come help me with the ten horse," he whispers to Kole who passes him as he makes his way up the beach. At the shed he folds a heavy canvas cloth into a thick pad and drapes it over his shoulder. Kole silently enters the shed, lifts the reserve outboard off the storage rack and places it 'just so' on Salanoa's shoulder. He picks up a gas can in one hand, a bollard of line in the other, and follows Salanoa back down the beach. At the boat he puts the can in the stern, the bollard amidships, and wades toward the bow where Salanoa stands patiently, the motor balanced on his shoulder. Kole climbs into the boat. They reverse the routine, Kole taking hold of the engine while Salanoa places the canvass pad forward, just aft of the foredeck. The two men carefully lift the awkwardly weighted engine into the boat and place it softly down on the canvas cushion.

Salanoa nods to Kole, climbs into the boat, starts to stow gear and adjust the trim. Kole drops into the water and heads back toward the shed for another load. The gear they haul to the boat is well worn and old, shows signs of good care. Rough edges are worked smooth, breaks glued, lashed, or welded, and rust and corrosion fought

104

off with thick layers of marine grease. The motors are old and reliable.

The boat, freshly painted, inside and out, a few strakes showing signs of repair, is old and nearly ancient by marine standards. Generations of family have sat on its thwarts, maintenance keeps the boat seaworthy. It is a modified whaleboat design, wide at the beam, clinker-built, with a raised bow to help it cut through heavy chop and swell. Aft it resembles a gig, with high, narrow, flat stern, and stern sheets. The engine mounts where a tiller once worked, the engine providing the drive and the steerage. Four thwarts are spread along its length, and floor-boards cover most of the bilge, gaps are open at the stern, amidships, and near the bow allowing for easy bailing of the bilges. The boat is less than thirty feet, having a beam just over seven feet, amidships and tapering toward the stern and bow. Her draught roughly two feet of water along the keel, amidships to stern, with freeboard of eight to twelve inches when fully loaded with gear and crew. It drops to below six when returning with a catch. Built for the open sea, taking the seas well, and forgiving of off center trim, the boat is often kind to them. Two sets of oars lie across the thwarts, fastened against the risers, as is a harpoon, and a long wicked looking gaff. Killing clubs, knives, an ax, a harpoon head, are stored against the risers beneath the thwarts. Forward of the bow thwart, lays the reserve engine, the anchor and anchor line, extra gear, additional fuel, food and water, and fishing gear. Catch boxes are situated aft of the third thwart. She is set up to move quickly and to hunt.

Kole brings the final loads, hands them to Salanoa, who stows them away, ties down the smaller items, covers the gear with tarps, ties them down. When it is done they glance at each other, nod, saying not a word, the white sand aglow in the light of a dark gray sky, the sea breeze light at their backs they walk up the beach toward the fale where Sauaso's wife waits with a hot meal and large cups of strong tea.

Unlike most other village fishermen, Sauaso proudly regards fishing as his life's work. He rarely ventures into the plantations, finds little pleasure in the mud and humidity, sees nothing special in growing plants. He is ambivalent toward village society, wary of politics, participates when necessary, is bored by the ritual and protocol. Salanoa and Kole are older, have been drawn into the cycles of the land, see their futures in the village as talking chiefs, follow the sea for as long as they can. When not out on the water, or selling the catch, they work on the boat or repair and maintain equipment. They have all seen too much go wrong too quickly and now trust little to fate. If the weather allows, the men fish four times a week, going out on Monday, Wednesday, Friday and Saturday. Tuesday they recover and work on the gear, as with Thursday, except near holidays, when they fish six days of the week because of the promise of quick money. They go to church on Sunday, sleep through the day, thank God for the respite, and respect the church rules. When the weather is bad, they work on their equipment, or maintain the boat; the needs never end.

They are opportune fishermen, as likely to bottom fish at night as they are to chase the seasonal schools of pelagic fish that skirt the island shallows. Almost all their trips are beyond the reef, deep-sea ventures requiring great skill. They fish by hook and line, avoiding net and spearfishing. The money is in the pelagic fish, the bottom fishing is consistent, with higher pounds landed. Chasing the pelagic schools uses fuel, beats down the men and the boat, and is more dangerous, while the bottom fishing is at night, often wet and always unpleasant. Fishing rarely means comfort or ease for these men, and they follow the fish and the money.

The men are all family; Salanoa an uncle of Sauaso, brother to his mother, Kole the husband of an older great-aunt of Sauaso, the daughter of a paternal great-grandmother. The relationships center around Sauaso's father, Palailoa, who is the village high chief, a leader in the district, and influential in the national assembly. He is greatly respected by all. When the Old Chief, as he is affectionately called, retires, the title and the rights and responsibilities it entails, will fall to Sauaso. However, such change is ten, or even twenty, years into the future. The son is the heir apparent. It gives him right to authority among the older men; and his diligent work, fairness, and caution have earned it.

When the two men return to the small cooking fale, they sit down, and Tofa serves them a meal. Kole says a quiet grace before they eat. Sauaso comes in a few minutes later and sits cross-legged facing the other two men. His wife places a food tray in front of him, and the three men eat quietly and with some haste. When they finish, they smoke, passing the green Grey's tin, the papers, the matches. across the mat. They drink another large cup of hot tea, relax for a brief moment, and prepare mentally for the trip.

"We'll head north of the islands," says Sauaso in a low murmur, " Tomaso says he saw large schools working just north," he adds, mentioning the other village fisherman who fishes the schools. The men nod, saying nothing. Sauaso decides their schedule, tells them at breakfast. They rarely question his choices. It is enough to be fishing. There is some talk about gear, a few quiet comments, a laugh about a village happening; the men are too familiar with their work to discuss it.

The boat is ready when they return to the beach. Salanoa and Kole have stowed the gear, and Sauaso has tested the engine. Kole casts off the mooring line, guides the boat out of the shallows and hoists himself in as the water climbs above his knees. Salanoa grabs an oar, poling the boat into the channel. Sauaso waits patiently as the men work the boat free of the shallows, into deeper water where he can lock down the engine. Salanoa looks back at Sauaso's gray form, nods an 'OK' as he stows the oar in its rack. Sauaso takes over, he squeezes the tank bulb slightly, pulls the starter cord, the engine firing immediately. The boat slips away from the land, becoming a dark form on the silvery dawn sea, sliding into the dimness, slipping out toward the reef.

The crew is busy with well-known tasks, carry them out smoothly and with deliberate care. Sauaso stands in the stern sheets, the extra-long tiller bar lays in his hand as he gazes forward over the bow, picking out the familiar shadows of the isolated coral heads studding the uneven channel. The surf is crashing along the reef; faces of six to eight feet build high before tubing and crashing in foamy violence. Sauaso slows the boat as he watches the waves break white across the reef opening. Then, deciding on the cycle of the sets, he guns the engine and the boat pushes and bounces through the white foamy breakers. Spray flies high from the bows, water rushes in over the gunnels, and into the bilges. Kole bails madly as they buck through the breakers. In brief minutes they are out and beyond the break, into the still boiling waters beyond the reef. The sudden violence of the passage lays muted behind them, the roar of the surf now a thunderous thumping.

Kole drops a line overboard, returns to bailing. Sauaso looks around slowly, taking in the pleasures of the unborn day, letting out a loud yell full of relief. The other men smile, their eyes echoing Sauaso's relief. It is good to be free of the land, back on the water, and ready to fish.

A fish hits the lure while the sweet scent of sea foam from the reef passage is still in their nostrils, the water still churned from the break. Sauaso slows the boat as Kole hauls in, hand-over-hand, long looping coils of monofilament lay on the decking, a silver arrowhead tracing the dark sparkling waters, darting back and forth along the diminishing arc of the line, a small Malauli, a jack, fighting violently as it catches sight of the boat.

"Kole, your dinner," smiles Sauaso—The first fish always 'Kole's dinner'—and good luck when caught early.

"Ahh," says Kole as he pulls the jack aboard. "It will fry up nicely." He grabs the killing stick, whacks the still fighting jack against its skull, laying it stunned in the bilges, foot cautiously firm over its body, removing the lure from the slack jaw filled with a razor sharp band of teeth, then dropping the pearl shell deceiver back over the side and into the dark emerald waters.

They head west along the reef, edging deeper, running just off the ridge breaks where the deep water jacks lurk in ambush. They head away from their destination, moving along an arm of the reef that cocks back toward the northwest. To the east, several miles out, in deeper water, lie the islets Sauaso seeks. The islands ride hard up on the eastern ridge, dark beads along the long arc of shallower water. The western arm curving back, aiming toward the northeast, pitching them into deeper water like a slow slider, just high of the northern edge of the last island in the emerald chain. They'll skip by, over into the deep water, where long running ocean currents run up against the shallow ledge of the islands and bring in the schools.

Their goal is the skipjack and yellow fin, tuna species, large schools of manageable sized fish, easy to fish, prized by the villagers. They are ready for anything, hunters of opportunity, men who will take a basking green turtle, a playful porpoise, or even a nosey shark. They will avoid it only if it is poisonous or poor eating.

They drop three lines, three cruising lures cutting through the green sea, skipping over the surface as the chop works them out, tosses them high, catches them and takes them deep again. Then a sharp twang on a line, the sight of the silvery fish running high in the water behind the boat, a broken crescent of light as it regains depth and fights to escape. This is a larger deeper water jack, demanding greater strength, and Kole labors as he creates a looping pile of line. The fish's power flashes down the line like electricity, charging the boat and setting the men on edge. Salanoa is ready with the gaff as the shimmery beast comes alongside, whips away at sight of the boat's watery reflection, is pulled ever closer, then the tarnished metal hook of the gaff smoothly slips into soft flesh, the large fish is hoisted into the boat, fighting in the bilges. fifteen pounds of muscle, fin spines, and razor sharp teeth, fighting strongly and far from dead, the jack ricocheting about the bilges until the men manage to club it into passivity, a final beating exploding bloody gore about the boat, painting the men in the colors of death. A marvelous catch and gutted and gilled before it is dead; eyes wide staring in glassy shock, the flesh still aquiver as it is slipped into a wet burlap bag, cooled into the afternoon in hopes of a good price when sold in town, at a restaurant, or to an expatriate wife.

Off on the distant horizon, almost lost in haze, the sun breaks over the edge of the world, casting its glare across the water, bringing paleness to the predawn colors. Brightness spreads, and Sauaso dons sunglasses and sticks a pandanus hat on his head. The long sleeves, the neck kerchiefs, the hats, quickly becoming protection from the burning sun, their warmth against the chill air of the cool morning fading from memory; just as the deep green seas lose themselves in the depths of a bottomless inky blue ocean.

The boat, tiny against the open seas, heads slowly toward the northern tip of the farthest islet, slides over the rills of easy chop and across the long slow valleys of the swell. Sauaso remains standing, the long arm of the tiller bar cocked, fitted into his down stretched hand, his eyes scanning the horizon and the high ridges of the far swells as they surge rhythmically past. He has learned there is no place to get to before one hunts, outside the reef it is always the time. Memories of missed opportunities in the predawn ride out key him to always be ready, to always expect something to happen. With two fish already landed, he feels a good day coming, a chance to load the boat, and he does not intend to miss the bounty.

The swell rises with the sun, the morning heat charging the seas. The breezes are still offshore and wispy, the day trades blow intermittent, tame and relaxed, unable to decide how they will treat the day. In the east, scattered across the horizon, backlit by the climbing sun, orange, pink, gray, and purple cloud heads drift slowly down on them, the parallelograms of rain they spawn appearing infrequent and uncertain. He gazes along the northern horizon looking for signs of working birds, those clouds of frenzied wings that will guide them toward the schools. Salanoa, on his feet in the bow, grasps the anchor line, bounces lightly in the stutter of the stem as it cuts into the chop. He gazes along the shifting horizon, pitching near, then far, in an undulating movement over the ocean swells. Sitting on the second thwart Kole is busy cleaning the remains of the gutted fish, dumping it overboard, rinsing the blood from his legs, washing the gore from the sides, resetting the hand line, and taking care of the never-ending need to bail the water from the bilge. The men prepare, uncertain of the moment, knowing their inevitable rendezvous.

They move over an empty blue ocean, a vast liquid desert, with no sign of fish or bird. They are alone, the blue gray outlines of the islands offering faint assurances. There is the sea, the deep blue water, becoming darker and bluer as the sky brightens, the smell of salt, fish blood and gore, plankton, gear, and engine exhaust fill the nostrils. The sounds are of the engine, the spray filled wind slapping what it touches, and the water breaking at the bow, rushing along the sides.

The islands fade into a bluish haze that robs the shoreline of detail, and they appear suddenly far away. The men move along the empty rolling plain, the endless ocean uncertain what it will offer them as they play a game of chance. Their prospects look good, luck has been kind to them, she is often precocious, one misstep or bad turn, and they will suddenly be isolated, with no helping hand or much chance of survival. They know the sea willingly gives up her bounty, and the trick is to avoid being a part of the return offering to her.

It is always unsettling, the shadowed figure that accompanies them on each trip. They speak reluctantly, and only rarely, of this presence sitting on the thwarts among them, walking into their fale on dark nights, while they lie with their wives close at their sides. Misfortune slips roughly into punishing dreams of trips to the edge, places of their own special dread, bringing on sweats, drenching the body, sparking an ache of a muscle too close to the bone, the heart racing out of control; the clawing desperation of drowning deep in their own nightmares. Yet the sea sings a siren song they cannot resist, spins visions of a world they love, yet fear and must respect. Their unease wakes them too early in the dark of night, their minds scrambling to prepare to depart. They stumble to their feet, packing for the journey, sometimes only to fall awkwardly out of their ragged nightmarish dreams, realizing it is a day not meant for fishing. The chills rides down the spine. It hurries them out of sleep, even when soaked with fatigue, chases them out of their beds as their wives offer soothing assurances. The salty taste of yesterday's trip, still lingering at the back of the throat, makes the dreams difficult to flee. It calls them to their gear, drives the fixing and repairing, and obsessive care. And in the end they live alone, speaking a language only they know, their subtle gestures and words, marking them, setting them apart as fishermen.

Their world has not much changed over the generations. Life on the island, in the villages, has become peaceful, ordered, and determined. These men, who not long ago, would have been warriors first, and fishermen second, are no freer now to seek their destinies than their forbearers were hundreds of years before them. They are still of the warrior class, the battle scarred. They are the men who regularly fight for their lives, know the cost of the battle, see their fate in the names of men who have not come home. Yet, they serve the whims of their leaders, are captives to their family's welfare, remain, from generation to generation, holders of the knowledge of life's terrifying uncertainty. True, they face no knives, or the war canoes of belligerent chiefs, the village is still a difficult home, and the sea has its weapons, and has never tired of the mayhem, nor declared a truce, nor grown fat and content over time. For these men the battle continues, the sharp awareness of risk, edgy and cutting with each sunrise. And if they were to come face-to-face with their warrior ancestors, they would stand among brothers, men little different, toughened individuals with the same feverish look in their eyes, and they'd likely find killing men little different from the necessary slaughter of the seas.

The working birds appear out of nowhere, blowing in out of the ocean haze, clouding the horizon with swirling dark shapes where an instant before there had been nothing to see. Salanoa and Sauaso sense the presence almost simultaneously, Salanoa cocking his head to gaze back at the stern, Sauaso nodding, edging the rudder bar a bit to the starboard, applying thrust and nosing the boat toward the sporadic cloud. Kole, alerted

114

by the change in engine pitch, glances from his work, and Sauaso simply thrusts his chin to the port. Kole stashes the lure he is repairing, checks the lines in the water, reaches toward the bow and finds the water jug. He passes it back to Sauaso, who takes a long chug and hands it back with a nod. Kole turns and nudges Salanoa on the back of the calf, hands him the jug when he glances down. Salanoa takes a long swig, nods as he hands it back, his eyes leaving the distant birds for only and instant. Kole takes a long gulp from the jug, tightens down the cap, replacing it in the gear. The men are prepared as the first skirmish begins.

They hit the school suddenly, the cries of frenzied birds, the madness of their feeding, setting them on edge. The waters ripple, slipping silver shapes and large staring eyes fill the sea all about them. Everywhere the men look animals feed on one another, the bloodlust spreading into their souls, reflecting the spirit of the hunt, causing their hearts to race, their respiration to soar and the muscles in their groins to tighten. All about them bodies are pumped to flee, to attack, and to kill or die. Madness, panic, and the frantic need to consume, are the common interspecies emotions. The men yell and laugh, killing as quickly as they can. Time slowing while the blood runs freely, they join the dance of death, and fight to reap a mad bounty.

The school is all eyes and stripes, fast sudden movements dissolving individuality. It is a broad shoal of fish, stretching far beyond the boat. It is everywhere they look, large enough to alter the sea, easing the swell, and settling the chop. The liquid plain is covered in rills of moving bait, great schools of small fish driven to the surface, jumping high, Arcs of small fish fleeing beyond their realm, flying into the air, caught by waiting birds, falling in a sharp snapping rain onto the surface of a jaw infested ocean. Only their numbers confuse, and grant the minority continued life.

Beneath the bait shimmer the bodies of a countless mixed school of predators, Yellow fin, skipjack, mackerel, dolphin fish, an assortment of schooling pelagic predators, all mixed together, forgetting their species individuality amid vicious charges against the waves of bait. Below this pandemonium, lower in the depths, deeper in blue darkness, the sun glistening through the blue filtered seas, another plain of conflict spreads out, another layer of death lurks; its special predators larger and fewer, more organized, significantly more intelligent and cunning. Here the roles reverse, the seekers are sought, the takers fall prey to quicker, larger, sets of teeth, and as quickly as some are satiated, they are taken by the ravenous. Death sweeps randomly among the living.

On the surface, amid the pandemonium, in the frenzy to feed, lures are mistaken for bait fish, lines hit fiercely, fish wrenched from their place in the school, and the men, adrenalin pumping, blood pressure soaring, hearts racing, pull in their catch. Elated, laughing, and happy to be working a school so early in the morning, they smile and joke, miss not a beat in their place in killing machine of the boat. Sauaso holds a line, feels a sharp hit, hauls in and slings the fish at Kole's feet. Kole, his own line trailing, ties it off, quickly, then whacks the small yellow fin with a violent impatient blow from the heavy club, the fish, puking bait, blood, gore, shitting everywhere, lays stunned into quivering spasms. He seizes the lure, still in the fish's jaw, taking great care to avoid its row of razor sharp teeth, wrenches out the lure impatiently, drops it overboard, letting the line play through his fingers, watching the whorls of monofilament unravel awkwardly into the sea, then he shouts to Sauaso, who nods, as the drag of the lure is suddenly heavy again in his hand. Kole returns to his line, now weighty with a catch, he repeats the cycle, pulling in the fish, whacking it mercilessly, ripping out the lure, and dropping the lure back into the sea, always guarding the line against tangles. Salanoa stands in the bow, his eyes on the school, watching the birds move along the water, his one arm holding the anchor rope, the other jigging his line, which is suddenly twanging, heavy in his hand, hit by a fish. He hauls it in, calls to Kole who catches the line by the side of the boat, slings the fish aboard, cracks it on the head as it bucks on the floorboards, spines find the soft flesh of Kole's leg, Kole swears loudly, blood spays the boat, the fish lies quivering as Kole pries the lure from its mouth, tosses it over, pays out the line. The cycle is repeated, again, and again; this simple methodical killing of working the school.

Lines have short leads, no need to hide in the madness, even the birds scoop the lures as they fight for the bait, a half dozen overhand pulls and a fish is aboard. It cuts the time, eases the strain, helps prevent lines fouling each other, limits the looping coils of line lying in the bilges like thin wriggling plastic snakes. The wormy tangles are fewer, the landings more frequent. Blood and gore coats the bilges and men. The boat churns through the school, reaping its toll almost unnoticed and insignificant as the great shoal swims on chasing the bait. The killing is an elixir that spreads through the body, slips into the soul, filling it full, like a long orgasm. The men fight to stay calm, to kill with efficiency, perfecting their trade, controlling their euphoria, and ignoring the raw sweet stench of death's convulsions in the bilges.

"Ehahhh!" calls Salanoa, looking back at Sauaso, pointing thirty yards off to the port, where a large black flaring dorsal fin breaks the surface, a great black pennant, a huge flag of war, Xiphias Gladius appearing amid the chaos of the school. The Swordfish, the saber-yielding gladiator, the black knight of the sea, cruises the school hunting distractedly. They glide past the great fish as it thrashes its bill, tearing into the school, its killing abilities as great, or more potent, than the boat's. Lion passes leopard in the midst of the herd.

Sauaso stares silent, calls out to Salanoa, "That's a rare site! They don't usually come into the schools like that in the morning." Then the black fin fades in the distance, they continue their troll, the fish keep on hitting. Sauaso, stares back, forgetting the chase. Salanoa yells a warning. Sauaso has drifted from the birds, the school has moved on in the blink of an eye. He guides the boat back, gunning into the bait, and the lines are all hit as the bloody hunt charges on.

The damage is done, though the bilges are filling, the school is vast, and they could be full in hours, the high black fin cuts through the darkness of Sauaso's mind, digging into memories that lay like hot embers, covered in the dark ashes of forgetfulness, yet still scorching hot. If it were only a fish, big and dark he could remark its presence, and move on with the hunt. The sight of the sword stirs generations of memories, lays open the family soul. No aumakua this fish, no family protector in a dangerous ocean. The sword brings them no luck, bestows no peace or tranquility. It is the challenge, the enemy that inflicts pain and draws the blood of the family, leaving only nightmares of vicious battles, of sweat, tears, and vicious wounds.. Easier they fight their own kind than dual Xiphias.

Yet Sauaso stares back, reliving his battles, remembering stories of epic conflict, hearing the echoed words of an oath he uttered long ago. His body screams 'fish on!', pride and honor, emotions which mix poorly with the sea, sway him never-the-less. In an instant he decides, moves without hesitation toward the greater challenge.

"Ready the harpoon," he whispers to Kole. "The heavy line on the reel," he says to Salanoa. He pushes the tiller over, turns into the school, pulls in his line and orders the others to follow. In moments Kole sits on the thwart, the long wooden pole tipped with the knife sharp metal point and tied off to their best line; the harpoon stands seven feet tall, demanding its due. They move back through the school, all eyes searching for the fin marking their opponent. They see it at a distance, it moves unperturbed, dismisses their approach. It awaits their arrival, is aware of the challenge, anticipates the battle.

The sea kicks up as the opponents come into the ring. Sauaso whistles lowly, Salanoa moves aft on the starboard, Sauaso passes to port, Kole slapping the long wooden harpoon haft into Sauaso's palm as he moves into the bow, Salanoa takes the tiller, cuts the power and lets the boat coast through the school, the black fin coming toward them at a leisurely pace. In the bow, Sauaso raises the harpoon, waits for the moment, the fish aware, yet continuing to feed, daring the men to act. The harpoon raised high, Sauaso sights in, the boat sliding through the water as the fish turns quickly toward them. Sauaso cocks his arm, his muscles tense, he launches the harpoon, the fin surging ahead just as he releases, the point striking solid back of the head. It is not a killing strike. The fish surges toward the boat, its huge eye rolling out of the water. Time loses its pace, the combatants meet silently. Xiphias stares coldly as it rolls to eye them. The men nod to Xiphias unconsciously. The four souls exchange salutes of gladiatorial formality. Face-to-face, deep in their souls they feel the chill fire of the coming combat, and within each mind sounds the words "The Sea shall have her due."

<><>

The suspended moment evaporates in the bright heat of the morning, and the whine of the sudden surge of line from the reel at Kole's feet. Xiphias races past them, dragging the line under the boat. They fight to turn the bow 180 degrees, watch the line, watch the fish, and watch one another. The boat heads after the black knight, the line whirring out, Kole dampening its progress with a wet rag, fighting to avoid tangles and reel snags. Xiphias reverses, comes rushing back, and runs under the boat again, heads off toward the stern. They fight to turn 180 degrees, watch the line, watch the sword, and watch one another. The men realize the black bastard is playing them, and then it is gone, flying off as the line screams from the reel.

"Give us more power!" yells Sauaso to Salanoa. "Tension, give the line some drag!" he calls to Kole as he digs into the gear for a pair of leather gloves. He finds them, crusty carcasses of somebody else's hand, brittle memories of a past day's effort, he works them on, trying not to crack the old skins, fitting them to this new purpose. Then he grasps the line, letting it slide over the gloves, working it a bit to soften the leather. He tightens down on the line, feeling the strength of the fish, the power of his opponent, realizing more clearly what he has committed to. The line pays out, the boat chasing after the sword. Sauaso lets the line run through his hands as Salanoa points the bow at the quarry, keeps good headway as the men battle the problem of tension versus the line on reel. They can only let it run so far, they can only hold it back so much.

"How big you think?" calls Sauaso to Salanoa, both men simultaneously trying to work out the physics of the chase.

"Anywhere from ten to twelve feet. Upwards of six hundred pounds, could be as much as eight hundred. He's nasty, they are always nasty, and that makes him bigger and heavier than he will measure out when we get him close," says Salanoa, edging the line to the starboard as the sword heads into deeper water, away from the islands, into its own domain. They fall silent, the difficulty of the task sinking deep into the gut, testing resolve, causing them to approach the question of possibility.

"It's heavy line," says Kole knowing the silent thoughts, "Tighten down on him good, wait for him to surface and try to throw the harpoon, then give him a bit of slack. He won't throw that needle; it would have pulled by now if it were going to go. You threw true and clean." he nods to Sauaso, "It went deep, the point is a razor blade, and all three of those barbs are nasty sharp. I filed them all. We have him. He is ours. We just have to be patient," says Kole looking first at Salanoa, and then back a Sauaso. The men nod, feeling renewed confidence and strength in Kole's certainty. Salanoa lets off a bit on the throttle, increasing the drag, Sauaso turns back toward the bow, clamps down on the outward running line, as it tightens he feels Xiphias vibrate his tail violently. This time, they think, we have taken control.

The boat moves over the swells, the school long left behind, the line angling down as Xiphias dives deep into blue coolness, carrying the boat farther from the islands, taking it into the dark ocean wilderness. The men bake in the sun, are drenched in sweat, dehydration creeping up on them as they stare after the line. They are tense, edgy and irritable, waiting for something to change, their energy draining away. They feel themselves soften, poaching in the bright glaring heat as the sun moves closer, eyeing them intently, the sole spectator in the arena. They sit still at their stations, silently fighting the battle; waiting patiently for something to change. Xiphias swims on, mile after mile, defining his battle with the soft bodies above.

The main islands disappear in the haziness of the distant horizon, they move far from their fishing grounds into strange waters with unfamiliar colors, and swell patterns that mark the open ocean far from land. Yet the fish seems intent on carrying them farther. They wait as the sun glares down in an irritable heat, impatient, demanding entertainment.

They must eat, are worn low by their fast, realize they must prepare for the coming round of the battle. Below Xiphias senses their decision, thrusts madly to the surface, charges back toward the boat, breaches the water, rams the boat. The men fall haphazard into the bilges as the boat is pushed over in the water. The water boils as the sword thrashes, its huge body pulling firmly against harpoon and line. In the critical moments Sauaso gives the beast his run, putting drag on the line forcing him to pay for his attack, the harpoon holds in the flesh, the fish and men remain locked in battle. In the excitement of working the sword, weathering its attack, they forget their meal, fail to drink, and slip further toward exhaustion. The fish takes a knight and dives deep once more.

In the early afternoon the men realize they must act. The fight wears them down. Salanoa turns the boat away from the fish, increasing the drag, attempting to slow the sword. Xiphias moves on despite the added weight. They discuss their situation, decide to take the tension to its limit, and move far out along the arc as the line permits. The line slides down the port side of the boat as the rudder pushes larboard. They wait, wondering over their next move, trying to anticipate Xiphias.

Down deep in the dark blue world, the fish charges on. It enjoys the strain, runs with abandon, feeling no fear of the men or the boat, and only irritation the needle dug deep in its back. The added tension is a challenge, the speed jets water through its gills, filling its body with oxygen, giving it power to charge on through the ghostly world of the depths.

Salanoa stands at the tiller, gazing out over the swell of a deep blue ocean, the brightness and heat surging heavily over him. His mind numbed by the sun's fury and Xiphias' determination, he drifts away from the task, thinks back to a time, still vivid in his memories, when he sat as a boy on the thwarts amidships, his father then standing tall at the tiller, guiding this same boat. They had hooked such a fish, perhaps smaller than the one they now face, it was a huge beast to fight and a terrible battle. They had been less well prepared, no gloves or good line, a motor less strong, less water and food. The men had been willing, did not shirk the task, and they had fought for many difficult hours, and brought the beast in. They'd hooked him on live bait with a light tackle for such a fight, and it called for all the skill his father could muster to keep the fish on, to tire him despite the thread holding him. The battle had cost, for the line had cut furrows deep into the palms of his father's hands, and he remembered the blood, the raw meaty look of the wounds, and his father's grimaces as he washed them in the sea. They'd gaffed Xiphias and near hauled him aboard when he'd lashed out madly slicing the line and slipping back slowly over the side, their hold on the gaff the only restraint. The fish staring blankly out of an evil eye and slicing at the arm of an uncle who stood strong holding the gaff, a wicked saber lashing along a forearm, filling the boat with curses and screams, Salanoa joined his uncle in holding the gaff, the struggle continuing, and he too being lashed, the wicked saber slashing deep across his thigh. Then, despite their desperate effort, the gaff slipping slowly from blood drenched hands. The Sword, as evil as ever, giving one last convulsive lash of his saber and going over the side, into the water, where he floated stunned, as beaten and as wounded as the men in the boat. He remembers it had shuddered just as a dog sheds water, the water dancing out of the sea, then slowly slipped into the depths. They had sat silent, considering their battle, gauging their wounds. Amid the sadness, the overwhelming feeling of loss and defeat, his father had stood and said a prayer of thanksgiving. They met the great beast, fought well to land him, nearly triumphed over the odds against them, and he thanked God for their lives and the day's lesson. Others would never have the opportunity to meet such a power, to humble themselves before the sea's greatness and wonder or understand how fear and respect were brothers of awareness. There was no defeat, his father assured the crew, in such an honorable battle as they had fought.

"We have caught other fish this day," his father had said, pointing toward the packed fix boxes. "We go home with a catch, and a memory of greatness. It is enough".

So they had returned to the village with a catch, and the story of a mighty sword and their epic duel, a tale of awe and deep reflection. A tale often told to men who looked on blankly, whose mind's eye could not see the wonders of the far blue ocean, and who could not cherish the mixture of emotions that comes from fishing the deep seas for its bounty. It was only other fishermen, their brothers in the life, who would pour out the drinks, and pass the tobacco, who would gaze into their eyes, and ask the questions leading to a retelling of the wonderful story of that momentous battle.

It was however, the last great duel for his father, for the cuts to his hands never healed well. The wounds leaving him crippled with near claws for hands; a man who soon realized he could no longer fish. His great sadness was tempered by the memories of his battle, the great duel he fought with that monstrous sword.

Salanoa glances down at the scars on his leg, mementoes of the injuries from the slashing sword, when he stood strong at his uncle's side, holding the gaff against the huge fish. The welts still sore on chill mornings, causing him to limp a bit. They had healed with great difficulty, festering and oozing. He was young, and fought the fevers and infections. Then the oceans and salt, the heat of the sun had been a salve to his body, sparking the healing, and he'd always thought he'd leached out the evil when he returned to fishing. These memories roll through the edges of his mind as he stands tall at the tiller, watching the line, his eyes a bit heavy, waiting for this fish to make its play.

Kole sits quietly on the amidships thwart working the reel, guarding the line against snags and tangles. He eyes the reserve on the spindle, knowing the battle must soon climax. He handles the line, his mind slipping away in the heaviness of the lids of his eyes, to relive his first combat with the Xiphias clan. More than a generation before, with Sauaso yet born, and Salanoa too young to step into the boat, he and the men's fathers had set to sea to fish as far out as they could venture. The boat then had a heavy keel and a sail, and they had hoisted it high, and let the island dip low toward the far southern horizon, the land slipping into the blueness of the ocean waters. The men sailing on, seeking nothing more than adventure. Out in the vastness, they had spotted a fin, the mark of a giant who basked in the sun. They slipped up on the sword as quiet as a cloud, and planted the harpoon deep and true into its hide. It dragged them off, taking them far along a watery path that led through the great dark ocean desert. They came off the wind, tried all the ruses. The fish swam on, going wherever it wished. Then far out in the ocean, after hours of travel, for no obvious reason, it decided to fight. Perhaps it had tired, or calculated its chances, or looked back at the boat, and realized its doom. It had breached from the ocean and begun a mad battle, taking all to the brink. It fought them for hours. They had heaved and pulled, and reeled in the line, then it had run out again. It was hauled back, their bodies near breaking, and they'd dragged the still fighting sword to the boat. Twelve feet of pure muscle weighing uncountable stone, a

126

monster, a beauty, a terror with fins. They beat it soundly with clubs to subdue it, his great uncle, the captain, insisting on a thumping.

"Pound the son-of-bitch to a pulp! Sure as hell he'll come back from the dead. I don't want that beast waking up swinging that knife!" The men fought on, mistaking his caution as fear of that devil, for they were worn thin by the fight, the hitting, beating, and bleeding. Then when the beast was still, they had hoisted him in, and the great fish had stretched across every thwart in the boat; its tail in the stern sheets, the bill near to the bow. They'd thought the battle was over and they were victors and heroes. They let their fatigue carry them off, collapsed on the thwarts, and slept with the fish, thinking they need only sail home, the victory feast already cooking in their minds. In less than an hour, when they were all drowsy, the fish had come back, risen from the dead or so it appeared. It had thrashed about the boat yielding its sword, ripping at men and crushing their bones. Legs had been lashed, spines dug deep, and bones broken by the force of its tail. The beast struck back, and they would swear the devil had entered that fish. It reaped a mean revenge, and when it truly lay dead across the thwarts, its evil eyes glared angrily, and a vicious look was engraved on its jaw. They had limped home a wounded crew, injured, uncertain of their victory, their triumph unclear. True, they ate the sword, and divided it out, but the flesh lacked the sweetness that such a grand triumph should bring, and was bitter to the taste; for their blood and their pain, their fears and frustrations were the spices flavoring that great-fish feast.

Years passed before the wounds healed; the memories of the mad battle they fought keeping them from chasing another great sword. Perhaps they had aged or the bitterness and fear had settled, drifted deep into the crevices where such emotions lie forgotten. They told their stories, remembering only the glory of the fight with the great swordfish. It became a heroic tale of how they had triumphed; the ragged wounds and the pain and the dread laying forgotten. In time the scars became medals they wore with great pride. And in the telling and the retelling a great myth was born of how honor was sought and bestowed in the battle with a magnificent fish, that giant sword. The true meaning of the fight; how the men had come together and suffered to conquer a great beast with a heart beating much like their own, how the fear, the blood, the pain, and frustrations, gave them a glimpse of the shortness of life, was left unsaid; yet haunted the dreams that still visited them on dark uneasy nights.

And the young men heard only of the greatness and honor of chasing the mythical beast, of the glory of bringing such a fish to shore, not comprehending what hard truth lay beyond the fine tales. It was a trap unconsciously set by old men who denied, or worse, had forgotten their fears, terrible pain, and that they had bled like the fish. They ignored the scars of old wounds, and the fact that through the rest of their years they had demurred from chasing a sword.

Kole sits on the center thwart watching the line. He nods inwardly, wondering if tomorrow he will remember the truths visiting him so clearly today and then questions if it will matter. He reaches for the water jug and passes it around, then looks for the food basket to feed the others.

In the bow, his hands on the line, Sauaso stands firm, guiding the battle, aware of the risks, accepting the challenge and believing he'll take the great fish home as a prize. "I am a fisherman!" he thinks. " I know what it means better than most, and if today a match can be found for the Xiphias clan then I am the captain, this is the crew and the boat for the battle. By evening we'll know if we are as good as I think. " He stands straight at the bow, strong and determined, immersed in the combat and taking the sword. His thoughts slip back to a time he sat on the thwarts a part of the crew. When his father stood captain and commanded the boat. They had hooked a great swordfish and battled him courageously for many hours before they got their first look. He had come to the surface, churning the waters, moving in on the boat, and attacking it viciously. It was perhaps twelve feet long, weighing perhaps eight hundred pounds. The old man had been honest, and looked back at the crew. "I'm not ready for this, and neither are you. Fighting this sword will take a terrible toll, and pound for pound the price may be too dear to reckon. I want us to be home at the end of the day and to sit whole and uninjured in church in the morning. We'll honor this fish, and that will be it. I'm not going to risk lives to catch this beast." So they said a prayer, and thanked the Good Lord, and then cut the Sword loose, to watch it run free. Then they went back to the schools and filled the boat with smaller fish.

The Old Chief was not sad to see it end as it had, saying "Killing is too tragic an end for such a great fish." Then shaking his head he added a thought, "And I've never cared much for the taste its flesh." Later in life, when he became a great chief, he often told the story of this fight with the sword, making it the hero to his poor fisherman. He told the tale with straightforward respect, and despite his failures and depreciations, revealed his wisdom and honesty.

Sauaso judged the Old Chief had done well when he cut that fish loose, for it had been more valuable released and living, than dead and an unpalatable prize. For Sauaso the loss was a painful defeat, and he rued the decision to set the beast free. He had vowed at the time he'd never back down. "A hunter hunts and he faces the challenge." He could not be happy without joining in battle, without taking that hard fought prize from the sea. So now he stood at the bow working the line, guided by the rules of his warrior code.

<>>

"He comes!" screams Salanoa steering a few degrees to port, keeping the line off the starboard bow.

"Kole, get ready, this is the run. We'll bring him in and keep him here," calls Sauaso as he pulls in the line, taking back what he had given, racing to keep the tension. Kole works the reel, recouping the line, keeping the bilge decking clear, ready to give or take as needed.

"He's going under us again!" calls Salanoa, preparing to maneuver in-turn, deftly goosing the engine, pushing the rudder over, bringing the line down the starboard gunnels as the sword passes them by, bringing the boat around in a tight arc, letting the line pass back up the gunnel, and head in the opposite direction The turn goes smoother and more efficiently than before. The men have learned their lessons and miss not a beat.

Sauaso pulls in the line, keeping the tension. When the fish races forcefully against boat and moves off again, he is ready to take the sudden shock, ease the drag, let the beast run once again against the line. Then he tightens down, feeling Xiphias surge, letting him know the final battle is near. Thirty yards out the water boils light blue, then erupts in foam and dark shadows as the sword rises out of the white mists, its body arching high, bill vibrating side to side, it leaps high into the sky as if to take flight. It is a rare aerial display, perhaps a sign of respect, a certain show of its anger, power, and strength. Then in a loud crashing splash, it crashes onto the water, and then sounds into the depths, seeking dark knowledge and power from the depths.

"It could eat the whole island," says Kole in disbelief, and no one disputes him, there is only stunned silence, which remains heavy among them, seems weighted down by their awe and amazement.

"Never seen one jump," mutters Salanoa with wonder. "Maybe twelve, fourteen," he continues, searching for a number to apply to the shocking vision of the saber-billed monster that flew over the swells.

"Not too big for the boat," declares Sauaso, breaking the spell, as determined as ever to land the sword. "At least let's hope so," he adds with a smile as the shock of the vision fades slowly from his senses. Then he is back heaving the line as the fish finds its depth, runs fast, makes a wide turn, and rockets toward the surface.

Xiphias charges in, eyeing them, sliding its jagged saber close to the hull, dipping under, rising and rolling an eye toward the boat once again, unafraid, almost relaxed, it greets the men, anticipating their actions, always a step ahead, set on defeating them in this deadly game of chess.

The boat pirouettes to keep him in sight and position. The men work madly doing their duties, cogs in the weapon of the boat. Sauaso stands, arms aching, his hands refusing to create the necessary drag, the line biting through the gloves, deep into his palms, causing pain and bleeding. His back is on fire from bending over the foredeck, into the swell, balancing, then pulling the line from the water, keeping the tension steady and firm. The fatigue reaches from his shoulders down through his lower back and gluteus and into his toes. There is no muscle he has not called on for extra effort. Sauaso has eaten little; a piece of cold taro, a swig of warm water. Now, deep into the day, it comes home to him, the weakness rising despite the endorphins that have soaked his body, charging him with strength, earlier giving him a feeling of infinite stamina. He wilts in the hot glare of the sun as the fight to keep tension on the line moves through the long afternoon. He fights on, willing his body to respond as needed.

Kole sits solid, unmoving and strong, guarding the line, reeling in the slack, avoiding tangles, spreading the line evenly over the spindle, always ready to pay it back out when the sword makes a run. Drenched in sweat, his back aches, his legs are cramping, and he yearns to stand and stretch. He is sore and stiff, the ordeal and his age each take their toll, but his experience gives him stamina, a deep well of strength gleaned from past Xiphias battles. There is no song to sing, or myth to tell, of a fight with a sword he has not dismissed. For him it is simply a dangerous battle for pounds of fish flesh.

In the stern, piloting the boat, Salanoa squints and gazes into the ocean glare, fighting to keep his eyes on the line, waiting for Sauaso and Xiphias to bring the battle to a climax. The welts on his leg itch and he glances down at them, reminded of another battle with such a sword and now ready to make a better showing, to defeat the sword.

The fish tugs violently, charges again, attacks the boat, with not quite the force as before, appearing less strong and determined. It sounds and dives with less force.. Sauaso lets it run briefly before tightening down again. He becomes intent on the play of the line through his hands, sensing the battle is fast coming to its climax.

The sword breaches again, churns up the waters and thrashes the seas turning them frothy. Sauaso fights the fish, the fish surges forward, they pull in the slack and give nothing back. Suddenly Xiphias seems played out and tired, his runs not so strong, nor as far, then he sees the boat and churns the water, appears too exhausted, too spent to resist. They pull him in, one foot at a time, giving a little, taking more back. Then the great Xiphius he is alongside, as long the boat. They look down in amazement, trying to decide just how they will handle the monster. It is a dangerous moment. They cannot delay. They need to subdue him before he revives.

"Kole get the gaff and secure him. Use the loop at the end to tie it off to the thwart," commands Sauaso. "Get the sledge and try to whack him. Bash him a few times just behind the eyes near the top of the skull!" Sauaso, in the bow and holding the harpoon line, seeks a place to tie it off. "Salanoa, try to loop a rope around his tail. Tie him off to the stern. Give it no slack until we get him quieted, I don't want him pulling us over if he changes his mind."

Kole, the gaff in his hand, reaches for a rope in the gear, ties it off to the gaff, then reaches over the side, and hooks the giant under the gill plate, pulling him close in a grueling struggle. The point of the gaff digs in, immobilizes the fish, allowing Kole to tie the long handle of the gaff off tight to the thwart bench. It is awkward, but it holds the fish deep and secures him. Then Kole grabs the heavy iron mallet and swings it forcefully down on the fish. It hits the water and the fish twists in agony wrenching the boat, near dragging it over. "Try it again, and in the same place, see if you can crack his damn skull," says Sauaso, the line biting deep into his palms as he fights to keep the harpoon line tight against the boat, finding it difficult to loop the line over the anchor cleat, the strain ripping his back muscles near from the bone.

The men carry out their tasks as efficiently as possible, the fish flexing and thrashing alongside the boat, its fins becoming vicious, its tail a dangerous weapon, the long saber near the bow looming deadly as it cuts and thrusts. They are overcoming, and taking control. Kole continues to bring the sledge home. Salanoa, in the stern, tries to loop the line around the sword's flexing tail. Sauaso stands firm in the bow still trying to find an opportunity to loop the harpoon line around the anchor cleat.

Then the sea jams them violently, a rouge swell throws them high, tossing them roughly. The fish is thrown up, and near into the boat as they slip back down the huge unexpected swell. It creates just enough slack in the lines, and Xiphias slips the gaff. Salanoa misses his loop on the tail. The sword is held only by the harpoon point, by Sauaso's strength against the line. The strain is sudden and so intense he cannot speak. He stands stiff and silent in the bow for an instant, before the other two men realize what is happening. Kole reaches for the gaff, finds he must untie it, and he fights with the ropes. Salanoa realizes the fish has moved his tail away from the boat and the opportunity to secure it has momentarily passed. He reaches for the tiller bar to goose the motor and bring the fish back alongside. It is suddenly happening too fast to control.

Xiphias senses the moment, and its head comes out of the water, the tail thrusting strongly, and the writhing sword rides into the boat, pinning Sauaso against the foredeck, the swordbill aiming at Sauaso's chest. Another mad thrust of the tail, and the bill silently slides deep into Sauaso as he stares down transfixed, impaled, unable to move, still caught in a death grip on the line. Xiphias stares at him through a large glassy eye. Then the boat tops another swell and the angles reverse, and the pain rushes into Sauaso's chest and head. He screams in agony as the tension rises, the bill flexing inside him, his chest crying to explode. Xiphias is rocked back, its weight heavy against the swordbill, the tension lifting Sauaso off his feet, and then the bill snaps. Eight hundred pounds of fish rides down the swell, and four inches of sword bill protrude from Sauaso's chest, still stuck deep inside him. He looks down to see the jagged lance protruding from his chest as pain carries him into blackness. Xiphias slips, ever so slowly, back into the sea.

Kole the gaff free of the thwart, manages to slip it home once again, but the harpoon line is now loose, Sauaso is collapsed in the bow of the boat. Xiphias stares through an evil eye. Kole has lived this before and awaits the sword. He looks back at Salanoa, who knows just as well, and who leaps amidships and joins in holding the gaff. The two stand aligned against the great beast hoping the pain of the gaff digging through its gills will force it to quiet a bit, they look at each other seeking a plan out of the sudden calamity.

"Get the harpoon line. I'll work the gaff. We need to hold his head close to the boat," gasps Kole through the strain. Salanoa is quick, and jumps to the bow where he grabs the harpoon line, drags the sword's head close to the side, locking it next to the boat. The fish has revived, it senses an advantage and somehow forces itself back into the boat, lashing and thrusting, finding Salanoa's legs; tearing them ragged. Salanoa falls softly onto the gear pile, next to Sauaso, who lays unmoving the broken bill sticking from his chest.

Kole watches the sword slide down the gunnel toward him, sees the eyes searching him out. He holds onto the gaff despite the danger, and only lets go as the fish spasms again, the bill ripping into his arms. The fish seems unsatisfied, flexing its body back and forth. and the port gunnel slides slowly under water. The sea rushes in. They are going over, turning turtle, to be dumped into the ocean. Then, suddenly, the sea is forgiving, the swell rolls to their advantage, and the force of the passing wave rocks the boat upright. Xiphias slides slowly back into the water. Kole looks down to find his arms deeply gashed and bleeding. The boat is half-full, the bloody water sloshes in the bilges.

The swordfish, its fury unspent, thrashes the water close by the boat. Having taken the men it goes after their companion. The beast charges the boat, ramming it solidly. Kole collapses into the bilges as the sword attacks the gunnels. He lays there watching and notices the harpoon line still ties them to the sword. He grabs the ax and chops at the line. The fish continues to attack the boat, raking the gunnels. Then the great animal is back in among them, the boat tips again, and water rushes in. A huge eye looks blankly down at him, staring intently, the broken saber spasming, cutting figure eights, the bill carves the air just over his head. Xiphias does not lash him, or the others who lie stunned and motionless. Kole wonders if it can make-out still objects, has a brain hard-wired for hunting the sea. Slowly the sword slips back overboard, as water pours into the boat.

Sauaso appears dead. Salanoa lies in bloody bilge water as it swirls about his mangled legs. He stares blankly out of glazed eyes, showing no awareness. Kole, bloody gashes on his arms, sits stunned, the water sloshing within a few inches of the gunnels. He realizes any heavy swell can roll them right over. He looks about uneasily and sees an empty ocean. Only the sun, now moving low in the western sky, has witnessed this battle, and it is already heading for the exit, the victor declared, the arena empty, the vanquished left to find their way in the night. It is another battle to fight. One weighted more heavily against them than the one they have just lost so decisively, thinks Kole as he looks over the shambles in the boat. He takes a deep breath and reaches for the bailer floating at his feet.

About the Author

M.N. Muench served more than three years as a Peace Corps volunteer in the Pacific. He remained in country as

 an expatriate government employee for an additional two plus years. Upon completing his assignment, he returned to Hawaii, where he obtained a Ph.D. in Agricultural and Resource Economics. He later founded and managed a successful software development firm.

He resides in Hawaii and has studied Hawaiian history for the last decade. When not writing he is an avid Ultra runner and hiker.

Blood in the Water is the first of his *Tales of the Islands* collections of short stories. The second is titled **Cycles in Heat**. He has also authored an historical novel set in 1790's Hawaii, **The Vengeance of Kahekili**. All are available through CreateSpace, and Amazon Books.

The Author may be contacted at:

mmuench01@gmail.com

Other Works by
M.N. Muench

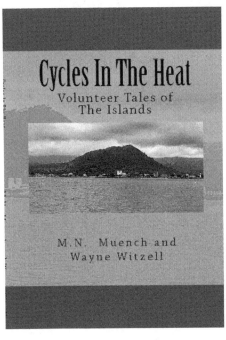

Cycles in the Heat: Volunteer Tales of the Island

In early 1971, President Richard Nixon was promising an early wind down of the Vietnam War. Yet young men died every day in battle, the draft was still in full swing, and the draft lottery the newest gadget to divert American attention from the war's increasingly bloody toll. The *losers* of the lottery wandered off to graduate schools or jobs in factories, while the *winners* found themselves taking pre-induction physicals and preparing to serve their country.

Among those contemplating service were two young men who found temporary deferments as American Volunteers on an island in the Pacific. One, an accountant, is assigned to work in town and struggles as an economic policy advisor, the other, a marine conservationist, finds himself in an isolated village far from town where he fights to establish a turtle hatchery. Both are overwhelmed by their environments, and are forced to deal with the inevitable difficulties of poor health and bad diet, frequent depression, an oppressive environment, and an overpowering island culture.

Here are seventeen edgy and often disturbing stories and vignettes that recount their experiences. These are not the Volunteer tales of tropical paradise one might expect. They vividly recreate the era, the tempo of the islands, and the cultural disparities that existed between young American men and the Islanders who called the shores home. This is an iconic set of tales that vividly and humorously captures the lives and loves of young men doing their service on the Island, while reflecting the experiential gestalt of the 1970's post WWII and Vietnam Pacific era.

CreateSpace eStore:

https://www.createspace.com/4208024

Amazon Bookstore:

http://www.amazon.com/Blood-Water-Fishing-Tales-Islands/dp/1482774763/ref=sr_1_3?s=books&ie=UTF8&qid=1405827835&sr=1-3&keywords=m.n.+muench

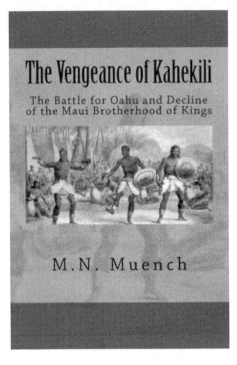

The Vengeance of Kahekili

The Battle for Oahu and Decline of the Maui Brotherhood of Kings

M.N. Muench

The Vengeance of Kahekili

This compelling and historically accurate tale is set in the 1790's Hawaiian Islands. Kamehameha the Great, having conquered the Island of Hawaii, is marshalling his forces for an attack on the leeward islands of Maui, Oahu, and Kauai. His main rivals, the Maui Brotherhood of Chiefs, fight among themselves on the island of Oahu fully aware of the threat from the east, but unable to quell their bitter internal rivalries.

When the English trading captain William Brown sails his ship Jackal into the harbor of what is now Honolulu in 1794 he could not have foreseen the terrible consequences. War had broken out among the ruling chiefs, and royal brothers battled for control of the island. Brown realizes his peril, however his ships need refitting, and his plans require King Kalanikupule confirmation of Brown's previous agreements with Kahekili, the new king's father.

If Brown achieves his goals, Hawaii is sure to become a British colony, possibly drawing the Crown into opposition with Kamehameha. However, Brown misjudges the impact of the war chief Kamohomoho, uncle to king Kalanikupule, and one of the few Hawaiian chiefs of the time who grasps the Englishman's mindset. Having fought a month long battle with his brother, Kamohomoho first maneuvers Brown into providing aid in the war, and when the battle is won, into an implicit statement of loyalty to the Oahu King. In due course Brown is called upon to demonstrate his loyalty, and when he waivers his plans are doomed.

Adding to the intrigue is the arrival in Honolulu harbor of the American vessel, Lady Washington. Her captain, John Kendrick, is no fan of the Englishman Brown and his intrigues and threatens their success. Also on board the Lady is a Hawaiian passenger, a young man known to both the crews of the Lady and the Jackal. Kavaialii, a descendant of Oahu royalty, has sailed to China with the Chief Kaiana, and on his return again found refuge in the service of Kaiana, now allied with Kamehameha on Hawaii. Kavaialii has come to Oahu on the order of Kamehameha to gather intelligence on Kalanikupule's forces and armament, and to seek out Brown's rumored agreements with Kahekili.

As the Oahu war ends, the fear of Kamehameha's invasion reignites among the Maui chiefs, and intrigue, murder, and plots form and unfold. The chaos of fear and uncertainty causes Kamohomoho to wonder if his brother, the dead King Kahekili, has not indeed cursed Oahu by seeking vengeance for past transgressions through curses against his own family and the people of Oahu.

The Vengeance Kahekili is the complex and accurate tale of the fall of the major resistance to Kamehameha's dynastic ambitions. It is also the violent story of the first Europeans to anchor in Honolulu Harbor. Well researched, highly annotated, and historically revealing, The Vengeance of Kahekili weaves a dramatic and exciting tale from the long forgotten facts of this critical moment in Hawaiian history.

CreateSpace eStore:

https://www.createspace.com/4098979

Amazon Bookstore:

http://www.amazon.com/Vengeance-Kahekili-Battle-Decline-Brotherhood/dp/1481822411/ref=sr_1_1?s=books&ie=UTF8&qid=1405827835&sr=1-1&keywords=m.n.+muench

37825856R00092

Made in the USA
Middletown, DE
07 December 2016